RED WHITE & BLUE

Mike Palecek

"Up A little out of place, a little out of tune
All I wanted was one chance
To let freedom ring
They said I had to get a permit
Tags and everything
I never made it through their red tape
I got this paper hat
I got a job workin' weekdays
You want fries with that?
I got nothin' to lose,
I got nothin' to gain
It's like a one way ticket to cruise in the passin' lane
I can't complain"
— Todd Snider

CWG Press

This is a work of fiction. Names, characters, places, and incidences are either a product of the author's imagination or used fictitiously. Any similarity to actual organizations and persons, living or deceased, is entirely coincidental.

Published by
CWG Press
1517 NE 5th Ter #1
Fort Lauderdale, FL 33304
www.cwgpress.com

ISBN 13: 978-0-9906714-2-8

Printed in the U.S.A.

Also by Mike Palecek

Fiction:

SWEAT: Global Warming in a small town,
and other tales from the great American Westerly Midwest
Joe Coffee's Revolution
The Truth
The American Dream
Johnny Moon
KGB
Terror Nation
Speak English
The Last Liberal Outlaw
The Progrrressive Avenger
Camp America
Twins
Iowa Terror
Guests of the Nation
Looking For Bigfoot
A Perfect Duluth Day
American History 101: Conspiracy Nation
Revolution
One Day In The Life of Herbert Wisniewski
Operation Northwoods: the patsy
Red White & Blue

Non-fiction:

Cost of Freedom (with Whitney Trettien and Michael Annis)
Prophets Without Honor (with William Strabala)
The Dynamic Duo: White Rose Blooms in Wisconsin, Kevin Barrett, Jim Fetzer &
the American Resistance
Nobody Died At Sandy Hook (with Jim Fetzer)
And I Suppose We Didn't Go To The Moon, Either! (with Jim Fetzer)

Most men, even in this comparatively free country, through mere ignorance and mistake, are so occupied with the factitious cares and superfluously coarse labors of life that its finer fruits cannot be plucked by them.

— Henry David Thoreau, *Walden & Civil Disobedience*

If today were the last day of my life, would I want to do what I am about to do today? And whenever the answer has been "no" for too many days in a row, I know I need to change something.

— Steve Jobs

The best fiction is far more true than any journalism.

— William Faulkner

PROLOGUE

We observe the continuing adventures of Red White and
Blue.
Good ol' Red.
Good ol' Blue.
Red White sits downtown on the bench on the side of the
street with the sun.
Blue lies at his feet.
Red says to Blue: Nice day, huh?
Blue nods and says, "I guess so," as Red's Adam's Apple
bobs.
Another older gentleman sits down on the opposite end
of the bench.
You have to let it all go.
Fear, doubt, and disbelief. Free your mind.
The sound comes from the dog.
The man leaves.
A woman comes. Takes a seat.
Again the dog talks.
I know exactly what you mean. What you know you can't
explain, but you feel it. You've felt it your entire life, that
there's something wrong with the world.
You don't know what it is, but it's there, like a splinter in
your mind, driving you mad.
She leaves.
Some kids come.
The Matrix is everywhere. It is all around us.
The kids jump off their bicycles, excited to hear the talking

1

dog.

You can see it when you look out your window or when you turn on your television. You can feel it when you go to work ... when you go to church ... when you pay your taxes. It is the world that has been pulled over your eyes to blind you from the truth.

The Matrix is a system.

That system is our enemy.

The kids crawl and shuffle closer.

But when you're inside, you look around, what do you see?

Businessmen, teachers, lawyers, carpenters.

The very minds of the people we are trying to save.

But until we do, these people are still a part of that system and that makes them our enemy.

You have to understand, most of these people are not ready to be unplugged.

And many of them are so inured, so hopelessly dependent on the system, that they will fight to protect it.

"Cool!"

The kids holler and high-five each other.

They jump on their bikes and take off, eager to tell someone.

CHAPTER ONE

"And in local news ..."

The pert man and woman smiled at each other and the woman took the lead.

"A man has been charged with domestic terrorism."

"Trying to talk to children on the way to school, in the morning, on a bright sunny day and giving them candy."

"And taken to the mental hospital," added the man.

The woman took the story back.

"The man was found sitting in a garage, along with his dog."

"It was surely not his garage," the male newscaster said, smirking, earning him a stern eye from his female counterpart, who seemed to think this should be her turn to read the news.

"And perhaps ... not even his dog."

She took it back again.

"A Mr. Red White," she said.

"Police surrounded the garage on Tenth Street, along with ambulance, fire truck and members of the state police after receiving a tip from local citizens about the man sitting in the garage that was not his own."

"Because the couple who own the garage had gone to Arizona?" said the man quickly.

The woman shook her head disgustedly.

"Who left the garage door open is a topic for another day perhaps?" said the man.

Seeming to be okay now with the back and forth, the woman newscaster continued.

"The man," she said.

"Red White," said the male newsman.

"Yes, a Red White," she said.

"According to police records, stated his address as The Rosewood Café."

The camera, in a two-shot, zoomed in on the woman to avoid showing the male newscaster laughing.

She continued.

"Apparently he has asked for a harmonica, to make the people happy."

A hand showed up on camera on the desk with a piece of paper.

The woman took it, read it and looked up at the camera, now again in close-up.

"Yes, there was a dog," she said.

The camera again pulled back to reveal the male newscaster again in his chair, putting on his microphone, straightening his lapel.

He looked right into the camera with a straight face.

"Red White," he said.

"Is apparently a fan of the movie The Matrix," he said.

The newscaster fought to hold his countenance, speaking slowly, forcing out the words.

"But ... he, apparently confused, calls it The Waitress, according to police reports that say he has recited passages from the movie while in custody."

The man became serious.

"We have also received word that this man, Red White, was handing out candy to passing children, which caused a major concern as we can all well imagine, to the parents in the neighborhood.

"He apparently enticed the children into the garage by telling them the dog could talk.

"No confirmation on that as yet.

"And, reportedly the dog went along quietly and not reluctantly when approached by a member of local animal control.

"This man's best friend doesn't get him either, it seems."

The woman newscaster, looking perturbed at her counterpart, cut in.

"And, again, if perhaps anyone would like to donate a harmonica, perhaps."

"Yes," said the man again.

"Mr. Bojangles."

"Dance," the two said together and smiled big as the newscast went to commercial.

Chapter TWO

"Red White and Blue! That's you, man!"

"You're a All-America!"

Red White sat in the little jail cell downtown with the other prisoners.

"That one commercial, how's that go?

"Red, White & Blue, we've got a deal for you," recited Red.

"Yeah! That's you!"

Red White did not deny it.

"They got you on TV, man."

"There you are, man, right there, see? In that garage, right there."

"There was shade and a chair. Nobody was usin' 'em," said Red.

"That your dog, man?"

"Yep, I guess."

"Where's the dog?"

"They took him."

"Where, man?"

"I don't know."

"Hey, man, there's you. What'd you give those kids?"

"Candy."

"You got any, man?"

"Yeah."

"Oh, wow, man, cool."

"Skittles."

"Gimme a Gummi Bear."

"Jolly Rancher, man. Thanks."

"You're the guy from that commercial, yeah. I know you. How come you're in jail, man?"

Chapter THREE

A ll the police office people gathered around the desk to watch him get released.

They stood around trying to look like they had things to do right there to watch Red White get his property back.

The woman behind the desk opened an envelope, tipped it up and out fell nothing. She tipped it up more and more nothing fell out.

"Where's my dog?" said Red White.

"What dog?" said a big policeman.

"What dog?" said Red White.

"Blue. That's who."

"Red White and Blue," said someone and they all laughed.

Red White had candy left and he put it out across the counter for them to each pick one. They all did and he popped the last purple Jolly Rancher into his mouth.

He waved on his way out the cold grey steel door. He squinted as he entered the bright sunny day.

Red White walked, looking for Blue.

He had seen them take him and he had seen Blue not putting up much of a fuss. He wondered what was up with that?

He walked past the same garage, the same open door, same empty chairs. He was tired and wanted to sit down, but he had to find Blue.

Red White walked past the old office where he had once worked, Red White & Blue Realty. He walked past The Rosewood Café, past his old home. He only looked out the sides of his eyes as he passed the places and did not stop.

He had been famous for having a line of glass bowls of many-colored candy out on the front desk at the office, and he had been famous at the café for having come there every Sunday after church with his family. He was famous in his home for many things, not the least of all his card tricks and lasagna. He'd been meaning to buy a harmonica. He heard they cost five dollars. He was anxious to show his wife and his children.

He kept walking.

He thought about the prisoners he had met.

"So, you named the dog after the Realty place?" one had asked.

"The business after the dog!" said another.

"No, I don't think so," Red had said.

"He just looked like Blue to me."

Red White remembered what he had said when his wife asked why he put out candy bowls like a dog kennel.

"People like candy."

Red walked past the house on Maple Drive.

He walked past the old realty office, and then The Rosewood Café.

He thought as he walked and wondered where they prob'ly took Blue.

He turned right, toward Burger King and McDonald's, because after that was the animal shelter.

Too much work.

Oh, he thought about it.

Sad faces, oh, he thought about it.

Everywhere, except on the people who were coming out of the bar to stand by the front door and smoke.

He hated rich people.

People don't hate anyone anymore. We used to hate the Dodgers or Yankees. Really hate. Now they are all like they're on the same team or they don't really care that much about the game. They try to like everyone for no reason. They try to smile and have a good day.

They should hate.

Red White thought about it as he walked.

Red pills. Blue pills.

That movie he saw late at night before the storm shut everything down.

Colored candy.

Two more blocks and then another right.

He slowed up a little bit because he wanted to think about The Rosewood Café before he got Blue.

He was in the café after Sunday church for Sunday dinner and the waitress kept smiling at him because he was the one who left the tip. And then she accidentally left a folded up crunched up piece of paper with the receipt and he sneaked it into his pocket and read it when he got home.

And that was when it all ended.

Or began.

You could say it either way.

That's the way they do today.

Most people wouldn't have even read the note. They would have called the cops. They are scared and too tired to read. They work and are barely able to turn on the TV before they have to sleep. If they could read they could learn and then maybe they could hate.

Okay, there it is.

The Animal Shelter.

The Great Man philosophy of how things change, he thought quickly.

He was a great man, he thought.

CHAPTER FOUR

Red White stepped into the animal shelter and heard Blue barking amid all the other dogs in the back room.

He was saying, "Hey, Red, get me out of here."

In the front, along with the desk and the waiting chairs were the glassed cat areas.

"I've come for my dog," he told the woman at the desk.

She asked him if he had papers and money and did he realize there was a fee for the pickup of Blue on TV at the garage.

Red said he had no money and no papers.

He walked to the steel door and looked through the window at Blue in a cage staring right at him.

"That's my dog," he turned to the lady.

"See?"

"I understand, sir, but there is a fee, and you need the papers."

Red White looked back at Blue through the window.

He looked back at the woman as she talked to a woman and a little girl maybe about a cat.

He walked in, straight to the cage. Blue barked and wagged his tail.

"I know. I know."

He pointed to the cage and the dog man in the back in the grey coveralls found some keys and walked over.

"Your papers?" he said.

"Oh, yeah," said Red White.

He dug in his pants and found a Jolly Rancher wrapper and handed it to the man, who looked at it and shook his head, then shoved the clear wrapper into his own pocket and fiddled with the lock.

Red White squatted and Blue rushed at him, knocking him over, licking him.

"Is that door open?"

He asked Blue.

"Yeah, maybe," said the man now putting the lock back on the cage.

Red White walked with Blue to the side door.

Chapter FIVE

Red White just stood there.

Blue lay on the floor at his feet, watching with one eye.

Red White nodded to the people coming in, some pushing carts, one's, two's, three's.

He waved a flag he had pulled from a display on the trip to the restroom he had taken immediately before anything else.

Most of the people smiled back at Red.

Some looked the other way, others too busy, intent.

"Hello, good morning, welcome to the store," said Red.

"What you know you can't explain, but you feel it," he said.

"What?" said an older man, maybe Red's age.

He came closer, waving a colored flyer in one hand as he walked.

"You've felt it your entire life, that there's something wrong with the world," said Red.

When the man got right up to Red and said "what" again Red shrugged his shoulders and nodded down toward Blue.

And then Blue began to talk as Red's lips fought to stay tightly closed and his Adam's Apple bobbed.

"You don't know what it is, but it's there, like a splinter in your mind, driving you mad."

The man looked at Blue and then at Red, then walked off, staring hard at Red, then at Blue.

A group of three women, with children, and three husbands trailing behind noticed Red White standing in front of the stack of packs of Pepsi to the ceiling, each of them nodding perfunctorily and looking past Red, over his shoulder.

One stopped, noticing Blue on the tile floor, resting his chin on Red's foot.

"Oh, nice," she cooed.

"You can feel it when you go to work, when you go to church, when you pay your taxes; it is the world that has been pulled over your eyes to blind you from the truth."

Blue looked right into her eyes and spoke.

"What truth?" she said, squatting, leaning forward.

"That you are a slave, like everyone else," said Blue.

"You were born into bondage; born into a prison that you cannot smell or taste or touch; a prison for your mind."

"The dog talks!" the woman turned to her friends and the men and children gathered around her.

"But," said Blue.

"You are all idiots, alas, stupid, fucking idiots, looking for the smart pills aisle and there is none."

The woman stood and led her group around the store, searching for the store manager.

Red White watched them and decided it was now time to leave.

He walked with Blue toward the closest automatic door and headed down the sidewalk, past the garden center and automotive, into the parking lot, the sun in their faces, so that when the frantic woman came out with the store manager and security they had to look into the bright light and could not see as Red White and Blue moved slowly out of sight, like a little ball in the sea.

They put their hands to their brows and scanned left and right, then turned and headed back inside because it was hot out.

CHAPTER SIX

"Oh, is that your dog?"

The woman buying minnows for her husband who was sitting in the car got on her tiptoes and leaned way over the counter to see Blue lying on the floor at Red White's feet.

Red looked down as if surprised.

"Oh, my God, I guess it is.

"How did you get *there,* fella?"

Blue looked up out of one eye, annoyed.

"We need bait," she said.

"We're going fishin'!"

"Fatheads, crawlers, leeches, spinners?" said Red White.

"Yes, those sound just right," she said.

Red heard the toilet flush way in the back.

"This may well be the only time in your life you can make a real difference in the world."

"You said what?" said the woman, trying to smile while digging in her purse.

Red nodded back at Blue behind the counter as he chased minnows with the little dip net.

"It's a waste of time discussing whether or not an aluminum tin can could penetrate concrete and steel for the simple fact that no planes hit the towers.

"OKC.

"Waco.

"Sandy Hook.

"Boston."

"I'm sorry," said the woman.

13

"What was that?"

Red White heard big, hard footsteps on old wood, dropped the dip net into the water, hurried past the woman, held the door for Blue and the door slapped just as the owner showed up behind the woman and asked her what she needed.

Chapter SEVEN

The two perky TV news reporters closed their eyes as their makeup artists fluffed their cheeks.

They opened their eyes and squinted into the bright lights and found the teleprompters.

They got settled into their seats.

"Well, here we go again."

"It seems."

They told about how a local man had been reportedly spotted at several localities posing as video store clerk, McDonald's, Arby's, Burger King and Wendy's drive-up window attendant, Super America clerk, Perkins dishwasher, fitness club trainer and casino bathroom attendant.

"And everywhere he went ... "

And so, police and everyone in town was on the lookout for Red White and the dog.

"The dog," said the woman TV news reporter.

"Was sure to go," said the man while tugging on his tie.

As Red White stood at the state park out on the highway and around some gentle curves, wearing his brown alien UFO ranger hat and shorts and brown boots, white T-shirt, with Blue a few yards away in the grass in the shade.

"These trees are old!"

Red White pronounced as he held his hand up to point out the forest.

"This river water is pretty old!"

He pointed over his shoulder with his thumb.

"Don't drink it. It's too old."

He pointed in six directions with both pointer fingers.

"This park was built and constructed a long time ago!

"Can everyone hear?" he said.

"Please come closer. Those in the back please move to the front, those in the front please move to the sides, those on the sides … please move to the rear, count to one-thousand-three and then return to the sides!"

Red White knelt down and petted the grass and made each of the members of his audience come up with him one at a time to pet the grass, then return to the group, either the back or the front, or the sides, whichever they had not already been in.

He then patted his thigh.

"C'mere boy, c'mere, c'mere, here ya go, fella."

Blue slept in the grass, both eyes closed.

Red White dug deep into his brown shorts and pulled out a purple Jolly Rancher. The crinkling of the wrapper seemed to awaken Blue.

Blue pushed up and so slowly walked over to Red, gulped the purple candy out of Red's open hand and settled at Red's feet.

"There are Bigfoots who live in this park," said Red.

"We receive reports from park visitors regularly. It seems there are a few Bigfoots families here."

The people in the semi-circle audience shuffled closer, trying to see over each other's shoulders.

"But see, the thing … "

Red's voice rang out like Lou Gehrig in the stadium.

"That people like …

"Is to find money … "

Some people in the group smiled.

"That's fun … to find money."

Red White held out his arms like a country preacher.

"This is THE United States of America!"

The people in the group looked straight at Red White and also all around.

"We live on lies!"

Red White sucked down a big suck of air and commanded the people to do the same.

They all sucked, big time.

"Lies are all we have going for us," said Red White.

"I wish I had a harmonica," he said to an old lady in the first row.

"Country music is so stupid," Red said.

He pointed to his ear and then to the people in the back row and they nodded.

"Just loving being poor and stupid and fishing from the shore – not rebellion and revolution ... it's stupid, and making songs about being stupid is stupid."

The words came out, but Red had turned his back to his audience. He turned around and the words continued, but Red's mouth was closed. He pointed to his closed mouth.

Then nodded down at Blue.

He put out his country preacher arms big again and had Blue speak a little Latin or Hebrew or maybe French, or just mumbo-jumbo Red was inventing on the spot.

Some people ran away in fear, others laughed and walked away, some laughed and stayed, some just stood there, not laughing.

Red White could feel Blue, resting on his right foot, getting pissed.

Red White held up a newspaper clipping that he pulled from his pants. He unfurled it and held it up.

"The Idaho Observer," he said.

"From your local library," he said a bit under his breath, as he had stolen the paper.

"The Blue Pill People," he said, in the midst of clearing his throat and it didn't quite get out.

He tried to stand on his tiptoes, elevate his chin and do as a real park ranger tour guide would do and then remembered it was Blue not he who was speaking.

He dipped his chin to hide his bobbing apple.

"With their painful life of working, and doing home chores all year, all their lives, with only a scant few moments of fun and pleasures ... "

One park ranger vehicle pulled up on the curb, then slowly others arrived.

Red looked at his clipping quickly, but he had already pretty much memorized.

"I've never seen a more addicted society to working and chores than the U.S.A. I hate working and doing chores, I prefer activities that elevate my body and mind.

"The facial expressions are the mirror of the soul of people. And see for yourself how sad the faces of most people of this sad country are."

A state patrol vehicle with lights flashing sped down the highway and turned into the park headquarters.

"Look at your neighbor, the person standing next to you, see how sad he is."

A fire engine blew its whistle and then a big red fire truck, ambulance and pumper truck pulled in.

"When gasoline prices rise to ten dollars per gallon, the price of bread to five dollars, along with extreme summers and extreme winters.

"Then, we'll see what happens."

The park rangers took away Red White's park ranger clothes, leaving him standing there in his white underwear?

We can only imagine.

Somebody pointed at the dog.

The fire engines and ambulance and state patrol and animal control took away Blue, charging him with seven counts of domestic terrorism.

Chapter EIGHT

Red White walked down the street, lined with trees and houses, fences. He walked past his old house and looked into the window and saw people that were not he or his wife or his children.

He turned right and left and stopped at a sign sitting on the ground, next to a garage next to an alley.

The long sign said "Red White & Blue Realty."

Red took one step into the alley and began to remember and then stepped as quickly back out of the alley and continued down the sidewalk.

And there was the restaurant, The Rosewood Café.

Red White walked inside and sat down at a window table for two and since it was Thanksgiving there were only some people inside and a waitress and a cook, being there because it was something they must do because it was this day.

Red White sat and looked around and said he did not need water or a menu, but that he just wanted to look around.

He turned all the way around to the big dining room where he had sat with his family when the waitress had come up to him and given him the note that had exploded in his mind.

After he was done remembering, Red White got up, waved to the cook and looked around for the waitress, then headed out into the world again.

Red White missed his dog, Blue, a little.

It was nice some times to have someone to talk to, and sometimes it was not as great as it sounds.

Blue was a reactionary, a counter-revolutionist, perhaps, sometimes it was hard to tell. Blue might be a neo-con, probably not an isolationist, surely with obstructionist leanings.

But Blue was something.

Surely something.

Whether he wanted to go break him out of the animal mental hospital was something else.

And how could he anyway? They would surely recognize him from the other times.

They would lock the doors. They would surround the place with ambulances and fire trucks and dog catchers.

That could happen.

Red White sat on the bench on the corner, an old wooden bench with an advertising slogan that Red White had never read on the backrest that was in colored paint but was fading.

From the bench he could watch foot traffic and automobile traffic. He could listen to the clicking of the traffic signal. He could also see the animal shelter and the television station and the beginnings of one street lined with food places, McDonald's, Arby's, Wendy's ... Burger King.

He saw the backs of the newscast team in the top window of the top floor and he could probably hear Blue talking if he wanted to.

And from where he sat he could remember everything.

He recalled the Thanksgiving Dinner of last year or the year before.

He walked in the front door.

He stood in the doorway until Blue could get inside, too.

It was chilly and the others gathered at the table stared at the door to close it.

Red White sat down at an open chair and Blue sat at his feet. He smiled around the table and everyone pretty much smiled back.

Red White filled his plate with the good things being passed around, some that had to come back where they had already been, because apparently Red was a little late.

He found an extra plate, put on some things that Blue liked and reached it down.

Red nodded and smiled at the conversation, the chatter, the football scores and assessments, the politics, the family history and news.

"So, umm, tell us about yourself."

Red White felt Blue's eyes and hummed with his mouth closed. He gurgled his Adam's Apple and pushed Blue in the side with his foot to get him to go stand where people could see him.

Blue stuck fast, dug his claws into the carpet and held on.

"Well," said Red.

"You've come a long way," some lady interrupted.

"Oh, umm," said Red.

"How is Aunt Ella?"

"Oh," said Red.

"I guess I don't know."

He took a drink and poured the rest of the glass on Blue's head just for spite.

"People like to find money," said Red.

People nodded and smiled and giggled around the table.

"So true. So true."

"Yes."

"We live in the United States," he said.

One person raised his wine glass and then all did.

Red had still a little water from pouring a lot of his on Blue's head and so he raised his glass as well.

The woman next to him clinked her wine glass heartily on Red's water glass and all clinked around the long table, full to the brim with stuff like food and napkins, silverware, candles and flowers.

They all drank.

Red kept his glass in the air and so after they had drunk they looked at him some more.

"Lies are all we have going for us," he said.

"Here-here," said one or two people.

"The moon," said Red White.

"We went there and never went back, how many years?

"Really?

"The same thing happened with the discovery of Las Vegas and gold in the black hills and Chinese food."

"I know, right?" said a young girl with a silver nose ring.

It wasn't too long until there were ambulances and fire trucks in front of the house, lights flashing, sirens running, both sides of the street.

That time they took Red White and let Blue roam free.

Sitting in jail, that's when Red White determined that Blue could do more than just lay there on his side licking turkey grease off his chest.

Chapter NINE

Red White walked into the gas station that had been changed to a big convenience store a few years ago.

He walked around the aisles, around the stacks of pop and the big muffins and the oil and Tylenol and nail clippers and Jolly Ranchers.

He grabbed a Snickers and a blueberry-kiwi-nut muffin, and then a Diet Pepsi from the cold window in the back.

He headed with his stuff past the line to pay, to the row of red tables along the window.

He sat with the guys.

They all played lovingly with their Styrofoam cups, looked up every now and again when someone said something.

Red White bit off a hunk of the Snickers and passed it around. When it returned to him untouched, he threw the rest into his mouth and crunched the wrapper in his hand, then started to open the muffin wrapper.

He swigged his Pepsi and grinned with his cheeks full every time there was a funny joke and nodded whenever there was something serious or meaningful or just something that was said.

Red White knew most of the guys around the table, though he had not been to coffee time for weeks, months or maybe years.

"So, how's the house business?"

One guy said in Red's direction and received annoyed looks from the others. He pulled his question back into his mouth by looking straight down into his coffee.

"Oh, fine," said Red.

"Just fine. You know."

"Yep, yep," said some of the guys and just as quickly found someone filling up an old car from their high school days and they all pointed and smiled, happy to put Red's whatever behind them.

Some stood to watch the old man out there putting gas into the old car.

The old car pulled slowly away and they all looked back into their coffee.

"You had a dog," someone turned to Red.

"Yep, I do," said Red.

"He's in jail again."

"You were on the news," someone said softly.

"Yep, I heard 'bout that," said Red.

"For sittin' in a garage," someone said.

"Now what's that all about. Ain't they got more things to do?"

"You'd think," said another guy.

They all shook their heads and wagged their ears like cows getting flies off.

"You're just all stupid as all get out," said Red.

They scowled and turned their heads, of course.

Red peeled off hunks of the big muffin.

"It's fun to find money," he said.

"We live on lies.

"I wish I had a harmonica.

"To make the people happy."

Red began going around the table asking each man where he had worked all his life and what he was doing now and what good all that work had done anyone all those years.

He asked them if they kept working while there were wars going on around the world and whether they ever considered that they should not go to work some day and do something about the wars and the poor around the world.

Red asked three guys that, the same thing, receiving no responses, only looks, stares, big eyes, teeth, hands white from gripping frightened Styrofoam coffee cups, exchanging looks with each other as if one of them has a bomb up his butt and the other guy is sure it's about to go off because they discussed it earlier that morning and he's not sure the other guy remembers.

Red White turned swiftly around and wondered out loud if they sold harmonicas here.

He turned back and saw that guys were chugging the last of their coffee, standing, digging in pockets for change to leave for the tip, finding hats, jackets, shaking hands, nodding, waving, heading for the door.

Red White tore off a substantial hunk of his muffin and found room in his mouth.

He washed it back with Diet Pepsi, shook one guy's hand and discovered an intricately folded dollar bill, and stared straight ahead, admiring the lettering and the traffic and the bird crap on the window.

CHAPTER TEN

The day was chilly and getting colder with the wind.

The town bustled along, trucks and buses and boxcars, little poofs of smoke, as on the cover of a children's book.

Red White walked along the sidewalk, on the edge.

There was plenty of room, but today he walked along the edge heel to toe, trying to walk in a line, his head down, arms out as if balancing on a high wire.

He wore his ball cap that he had found just minutes ago backwards in order to see his feet perfectly.

He stopped.

Turned the cap around.

He watched as a dog came walking, trotting perhaps, toward him, distracted, yet resolute, prob'ly in a hurry.

The dog, nose to the grindstone, headed the opposite way down the sidewalk.

It stopped and looked up.

A tear came to Red White's eyes.

Ol' Blue, he thought or said out loud.

"You escaped."

Blue looked behind him.

"What's that, boy?"

Yes, but they are after me, he seemed to be saying.

"There are no muffins or Diet Pepsi at Quick Stop," said Red White.

"I am off to Sudden Stop."

"Aliens," Blue seemed to say.

"They mess with us, take muffins, soft drinks, hide things. Soon it will be too much for us, alas."

Red White had not the courage at this moment to say that he had actually been banned from Quick Stop for the foreseeable future.

Red White knelt on one knee and raised his hand to pet Ol' Blue.

"Good Ol' Blue, ol' dog," he hummed.

Really?

Seriously?

Said the look in Blue's right eye with the raised eyebrow that he had seemed to have copied from Saturday Night Live when it was good years ago and Red White and Blue had watched it in his office at the Realty after working late at night and there was no reason to go home just yet.

Just move, Red White inferred.

Red turned and went along in Blue's direction.

They crossed streets and lawns and went down an alley, ducking inside a garage for a moment when a police car passed.

Red felt an old nail in his back and smelled the familiar dust and oil and gasoline.

A tear again slid down his cheek.

As his eyes adjusted and the police car crunched down the alley one step at a time, gun drawn, Red saw the old Sinclair Dino The Dinosaur sign, and there were the black and white photos that were not allowed in the house of his dad and his friends tipping over an outhouse, drinking beer on the wooden steps of the gasoline station, standing with their chins and chests sticking out, holding their shotguns and a string of pheasants.

Red White made his way around the old dusty car to a shelf on the wall. He picked up the old harmonica, wiped off the old dust, put it to his mouth and hummed softly on the low end, pushing away to cough up the dust.

He recalled his father sitting right here in this garage, the overhead door open, on wooden chairs with his friends. He would play and everyone would love him for it. All the neighborhood children gathered 'round in the alley, playing to the tune of the harmonica, chasing fireflies with canning jars.

And after the children had to go to bed, Red White stuck his nose into the screen in his bedroom and listened to the inaudible hum of his father still talking to his friends, telling them the truth about everything, because that's who his father was.

Who is in the house now?

Who knew?

"Let's go," Red White said to Blue as he put his dad's harmonica back where it went.

Red White and Blue exited the garage, slowly at first, peaking out the back door, Red up high and Blue down low, looking for a particular police car.

Convinced they were in the clear, Red marched off down the alley.

Blue trotted along, having to go a little faster than usual today for some reason.

He followed Red's feet down the alley, down the sidewalk, across a street, glad that the car stopped.

Blue paused on the other side at a patch of clover, shoving them, pushing them around, perusing, then just as quickly as he left the clover he sniffed an ant hill, huffing, sneezing as a few ants clung for dear life to his nose.

They continued down the sidewalk, stopped at a corner, and then proceeded again across the street, down this one block they had never been on before, perhaps, with lots of leaves, for one thing.

They stopped in front of cement steps.

Blue looked up and saw Red White staring up at a church as if wondering what to do now.

Red leaned down low and picked up something shiny.

Red opened the cellphone, a flip type.

He smiled and looked down at Blue.

"Yep-yep-yep," Red said.

"Uh-huh-uh-huh-uh-huh."

Someone passing on the way up the cement steps stared at Red White.

"One of my secret missions I'm on," Red White said right to the man, then flipped the phone closed and shoved it into his pocket, staring at the man to push him up the steps and into the big wooden doors.

The man pulled on the door. It would not budge.

"Aliens," said Red White.

"They do that to mess with ya, sometimes. ...

"... I've noticed."

The man stared hard at Red White and tried the handle of the other wood door, hurried inside.

Red White and Blue caught just a hint of the music and hub-bub and incense inside as the door was open, then just as quickly all was silent again 'cept for the hurrying of the leaves over the cement.

Red bent and returned the phone to the sidewalk.

He marched up the steps and waited for Blue at the big wooden doors.

They shuffled inside.

Red White held the door so it wouldn't bang.

They slid to the back pew.

Blue sat in the aisle.

"I found your phone outside, sir."

A young man whispered and handed the cell phone to Red.

Red set the phone on the seat and plopped to his knees, put his folded hands to his mouth, closed his eyes and bowed his head.

"I need to be forgiven," he hummed.

Someone stared at him from the side and he felt the cap on his head. He swiped it off and rested it on Blue's head for safe-keeping.

The minister came out and everyone stood, then sat, Red slightly out of sync, but he got set down with everyone else.

Blue lay in the side aisle, the cap over his eyes, his tail wrapped around him for a cover.

The minister stood behind the lectern giving the announcements of the day, the ladies club raffle and bake sale, the men's club poker night fundraiser.

He then asked everyone to turn to the opening hymn.

Red White reached for his song book, scooted over to check on Blue and see if he wanted to sing and noticed that Blue was not there.

Red looked around in back, stuck his head into the aisle and saw Blue's tail and his hind end way up there toward the front of church.

Red White stood and was told to sit down by four people.

He sat and sat as straight and high as he could.

He saw Blue on the altar.

Blue must have awakened from a deep sleep wondering where he was. He might have heard the minister's voice and thought it was Red up there and went to it.

And now ol' Blue found himself in church, up in front and not knowing what to do.

He must be in a panic, thought Red.

Some people snickered, some pointed at the funny dog on the altar.

The minister watched their pointing fingers and they led him to the dog standing right next to him.

He smiled and chuckled.

He bent down to pat Blue on the head and Blue showed him his teeth.

The minister stood straight up, concerned, looking around for the owner of this particular dog.

He felt a wet, firm poke in his calf as Blue nudged him, again, again.

With innate dog-knowing Blue sensed the minister's vulnerability, and pushed his nose against the minister's bad knee, forcing the minister away from the podium.

With the preacher out of the way Blue bent low and lunged, leaped, got his front paws up to the lectern and held on, looking around the crowded church for Red White, searching right and left, making direct eye contact.

Blue looked out at the people with those big ol' eyes. Red White could see that Blue had things on his mind, stuff he wanted to say to the people.

He pushed to the edge of his pew and stepped low into the aisle. He crept down the aisle, down, down, until he found an open spot at the end of a pew, almost right up in front.

Good Ol' Blue still wore the cap with the sports team logo, clinging to his ears.

"I s'pose you're all wondering why I've ..."

Red White and Blue began.

"Woof! Woof!"

Blue barked loud upon hearing the voice of his friend.

"You are all such hypocrites."

"Woof, bark!"

Blue pulled himself up higher onto the podium.

The people seemed occupied, so the minister sat down in his velvet-padded chair, crossed his legs and folded his hands in his lap.

The people fanned themselves with the church newsletter.

The ushers in back opened the big wooden doors for some air.

"You see graveyards all around you, but you act as if you will never die, with your TVs and your Happy Meals and your hot baths.

"Woof!

"You are sitting at the baseball game, so bored, so lonely, and then the damn television camera goes on you and you wave and smile and laugh and are just so happy. What the fuck, people?

"Woof-woof!"

Blue looked back at the minister as if to say he was wrapping up.

The minister smoothed his vestments and uncrossed his legs.

Now Blue barked loud, throwing out spittle onto the front three rows.

"Woof! Woof-woof!

"Bark.

"Bark.

"Bark! Woof!

"Bark."

He licked his lips with his giant tongue, pushed off the lectern and hit the floor with the clack of his front paws, turned and trotted up the aisle as the minister approached the podium and asked the people to please turn to page eighty-two in the new song books and thanks goes out to the Wednesday Club for that.

Red White and Blue pounded down the outside cement church steps and behind them came the young man in white shirt and black pants, black shoes.

Red ran, Blue ran.

The young man ran after them, holding up the cell phone like the liberty torch.

CHAPTER ELEVEN

Red White stood in line at the job service office.

And then he got up as far as the silver pole that held the black ropes that ran around and around and formed the zig-zag line.

He shuffled around the rope maze. He watched the clock, watched the office people working. He listened to the people in front of him talking and also to the people behind him.

His stomach rumbled.

And then he was the first one in line.

He looked back at all the people behind him, around the zig-zag and felt glad that he was not way back there.

Blue lay on the sidewalk by the glass front doors, watching with one eye open the people going inside.

Red White watched, his papers in his hands, the four possible cubicles he might be called to.

His eyes scanned back and forth like radar, and his heart sent out sonar pulses.

A man in a blue shirt and blue tie stood and shook the hand of a man wearing a red bandana. The man in the red bandana hurried to grab a cigarette from his pocket as he headed for the door.

The man in blue shirt and blue tie sat down, wrote something, typed something, then stood and walked up to Red White and reached out his hand to shake.

Red handed him his card and papers and followed him to the cubicle.

Red White and the man in blue sat in chairs on opposite sides of the desk.

The man began working a checklist, asking Red White silly questions.

Red tried not to laugh.

The man noticed Red's amusement and asked Red if he would like some coffee and if Red was feeling okay.

Red said, "No, yes."

The man kept going, making marks on his paper and looking up to ask Red the funny questions.

"It says here you have ..."

Red was looking away, watching a pretty woman worker walk past and was not really listening.

"Mr. White," said the man in the blue shirt and the blue tie.

"It says here that you have not worked in the past ..."

The man made subtle calculations with his fingers.

"A long time," said Red White.

"Yes," said the man.

"Why?"

"Oh, just cuz, I guess," said Red White.

"Red White & Blue Realty," said the man.

"Tell me about that."

"Not much to tell," said Red.

"You know what Realty means, right?"

The man nodded.

"It's pretty much over. The sign's down on the ground."

The man made serious faces with his mouth and nose and eyes and wrote on his paper.

He looked up, very sincerely.

"How would you describe yourself?"

"I really wouldn't," said Red.

The man looked down to write and to type, then looked again at Red, eye to eye.

"What would you say is your greatest strength?"

Red looked up and to the right to think.

"Pro-ba-bly, my legs," he said.

The man looked around the desk, and then wrote and typed and looked at Red again.

"Your greatest weakness?"

"My hands," said Red.

"I can't really open things like peanut butter like you would think a guy could."

"How do you work with others?"

"Well, they do some things and I do some things, and if I do it right, they do more."

Red spoke slowly so the man would understand.

"What motivates you?"

"Constant loud yelling. I really jump."

"Do you prefer to work independently or as a team?"

"Well, I prefer not to work at all. Don't you? But if I have to, well, if the other guy, you know, does more, well, you know, then I'm not too tired later to do something I actually want to."

"If you could re-live the last ten years of your life, what would you do differently?"

Red's face blushed.

He leaned forward and whispered that he too believed in time travel.

The man in the blue tie stared at Red White, and Red White sat back in his chair.

He looked down, at the floor, at his hands, then back up at the man.

"Well, prob'ly I would eat more than I did the first time. I wouldn't worry so much, as much, about carbs."

He looked around.

"Can you swear in here?"

The man subtly nodded.

Red leaned forward into the desk, folded his hands very sanely on the desk as if they were discussing all the things Red had brought to the table.

"I'll tell you what," Red said.

"I wouldn't have read that note from the waitress, for one thing. I'll tell you that.

"Dammit," he whispered and leaned forward a smidge.

Red paused.

The man took his cue and wrote something on his paper.

The man stopped writing and stared at his paper, then looked up at Red.

"Mr. White, can I be candid?"

Red nodded, saying, "Don't you mean, may I?"

"Why are you so different?"

He emphasized the last word as if, if he said it too loud it would detonate a bomb in his butt.

"I have your whole life in my hands. Right now. Your whole life."

"I am not afraid of you," said Red right away.

"My *whole* life is not *that* big a deal."

The man's countenance displayed that Red's time was up.

"Choosing to be one who understands, not one who remains in la-la land," said Red quickly, looking to the right and up to remember the line.

He looked around at the man's work place.

"I mean, really?" said Red softly.

He stood and shook the man's hand at the same time, thanked him for his time, left his card and papers on the man's desk and headed for the door, hurrying past the young man holding up the cell phone, trying to get Red's attention while noting the long line and congratulating himself on not still being there at least.

Chapter TWELVE

Blue followed Red as he left the employment office.
On the next street they saw a crowd and headed for it.

They pushed through the people toward an open spot on the curb where Red sat.

Blue lounged in the street at his feet.

The high school band marched past and the twirling club.

Three semi trucks blew their horns loud and some little fat shit wearing a paper U.S.A. hat fired hard candy at Red White and Blue.

Blue opened one eye after being hit on the forehead by something golden.

The candy lay all around them like bread crumbs at the zoo for blind geese.

Next came the clowns driving the little cars, then some politicians in open cars waving.

Then flags and soldiers and people with cans and tiny flags collecting money for the soldiers now coming in wheelchairs.

Red got up and headed right between them, followed by Blue.

Red walked up the steps to the reviewing stand.

Red sat in an open chair in front of the microphone.

Blue stood and barked at the poodle club passing.

Red crossed his legs and folded his hands in his lap, reached his cap from Blue's head and put it on, tugging the bill down against the sun.

As the Hometown Realty float approached, Red uncrossed his legs, dusted himself off and stood.

He walked to the microphone and began to address the town.

He told them about the transgressions of Hometown Realty, how the owner drinks and goes out behind his wife's back.

"Mr. Tuttle, if that is his real name," said Red.

"Cannot button his top button, not for years.

"He is a fat, fat fatty.

"And there he is!"

Red pointed.

Some people snickered, some looked annoyed. The rest looked puzzled and many did not hear him, so accustomed were they to the droning of the parade announcer, for years announcing trucks, horses, bands, miniature cars, and flags.

Red White stepped up tight to the stand and gripped it, put his mouth right on the microphone.

"Those clowns are not really funny," he droned.

"Really?"

He waited, watching the clowns watching him.

"The band from Mt. Pleasant, though plucky, is out of step and the entire clarinet section is on work release," said Red.

"Our parade queen is ugly, chubby, obviously chosen as a favor to her father the banker and because nobody else wanted it.

"This candy is not special. You can buy more fresh stock in the store right behind you.

"Those twirlers are precious, that is true. Never get tired of those, but whoever painted on all that lipstick should have just purchased a giant doll online instead of having children.

"Those soldiers are murderers. They are not protecting anyone. They steal from you so they can go plunder others. You all know that.

"And, finally, whoever decided it's a great idea to have horses come down our streets to shit and piss and bring flies and leave disease because horses are so rare and stunning, well, you are an idiot and should be elected mayor, then shot in the knees by midgets wearing camo behind your desk as you walk in the door on your first day."

By now there were clowns and soldiers and band leaders, and moms, pushing against the reviewing stand, pointing and screaming at Red White, along with the young man holding up the cellphone as high as he could in the midst of the throng.

"Booo!"

"Shut up!"

Blue tugged on Red's pant leg as a herd of green and yellow tractors inched down the street, squeaking, puffing.

Red White hurried down the steps as Blue made room by growling, baring his teeth, barking, snapping.

Blue cleared a path through the angry crowd, back across the street.

He nudged Red White into Stub's Place and then pushed him through the dark bar, smelling of sweet beer and cigarettes, past the pool tables and ammonia-eye-burning-smelly restrooms to the back door.

Blue shoved the screen door open and they stood in the alley, Blue panting, Red shading his eyes against the bright sun.

They heard angry crowd-like shouts coming from inside the bar and saw an angry mob at the end of the alley, now seeing them, pointing and heading their way.

Blue woofed at Red and nodded, this way, and darted down the alley.

Red moved as hastily as he could, barely keeping up, following Blue into the alley back door of a shop.

Soon they were smack in the middle of a jewelry store.

Blue's tail whapped a green Tiffany lamp and Red caught it just before it crashed into a million thousand-dollar pieces.

They walked, inched, trying to appear to stroll, between the glass cases of rings and watches and necklaces.

"How may I help you?" said a man in a perfect suit with perfect hair and nails on display behind a perfect glass case.

"Yes," said Red.

"Do you have any Grey Poupon?"

"Nooo," said the man, looking annoyed.

Blue pushed his wet nose into a window in the direction of a gold and emerald pendant.

"We're just looking," said Red, "thank you."

He stopped.

"Umm, wait, where are your harmonicas?"

The man smiled.

"Let me know if I can be of any assistance," he said.

Blue led Red down the aisle to the front door and out again onto the main street sidewalk.

Blue headed for a familiar place, the spot on the sidewalk where he had waited for Red at the unemployment office.

Blue plopped right down, closed his eyes, pretending to be asleep, implying that Red do the same.

However, Red, instead, opened the door and held it for a young woman, then followed her inside just as a branch of the angry mob ran past down the street with bicycle chains and tire irons, spatulas, fly swatters, a cellphone, and rope.

The man from the jewelry shop appeared on the sidewalk and pointed Red's way.

Red got in line, but it was so crowded in the office he was just barely inside the door.

He stretched his neck and noticed the cubicle where he had been interviewed sat empty.

He looked for the man in the blue shirt and blue tie and did not see him.

Red White pushed out of line, skirted the rope maze and walked up to the front.

He entered the open cubicle.

Red picked up the photo on the desk with the blue shirt and blue tie man in the same shirt and tie with his family at the beach.

He read part of the plaque on the flimsy wall as he sat in the unstable rolling chair.

Red touched the papers, the keyboard, adjusted his cap, smoothed his brown cargo shorts, pulled up his socks, looked to see who was next in line.

He got up again and walked up to the older man, fine white hair, trim white mustache, wearing a suit, gripping a briefcase.

Red White recognized the man as having once been a local banker, a loan officer, the loan officer, perhaps, who had had something to do with Red's last attempt, hurrah, it was a long time ago.

"Hello!"

Red gripped the man's hand.

"How are you?

"Please, come with me."

They entered the cubicle.

Red talked about the weather and the baseball and the football and the golf.

He asked for the man's papers and card.

He touched the computer keys and as the man leaned forward to see what had appeared on the screen, Red turned the computer slightly away.

"Please, sir," he said.

"Secret stuff."

The man sat back, setting his briefcase in his lap.

"Well, umm," said Red.

"Nice day, could rain, maybe not.

"I hope not!"

He said as he rose to a squat and high-fived with the man, a Mr. Sterling.

Red returned to his chair, placed his hands on the desk and found he was staring at a list of questions.

He crossed his legs, leaned back in the inexpensive chair, caught himself from falling back by subtly catching his balance by grabbing the desk with his toe that stuck out the end of his tennis shoe.

He peaked over the top of the piece of paper with the interview questions at Mr. Sterling like a relief pitcher at a batter in the ninth inning.

"Sooo, a Mr. Sterling," he said.

A Mr. Sterling began to look uncomfortable.

Red began to feel confident.

"How many hours a day do you put into your work?" Red said.

Red waited as long as he could, but could not help himself, even as the man began to speak.

"About half, right?" said Red, again rising to high-five, to which the man complied.

"Trick question right off the bat," said Red.

He ran his finger down the list.

"Hey, here's one," he said.

"Tell me about a time when you built rapport quickly with someone under difficult conditions," said Red, quickly changing crossed legs, banging the desk, exchanging looks with the next persons in line like a lion tamer to tell them to stay the fuck back.

"Yes, yes, yep," Red said, trying to listen to what a Mr. Sterling was saying while trying to find a good next question with his pointer finger.

Before the man had finished Red began the next question, feeling the need to say something because the office had just now become even more crowded and agitated upon the entrance of several of the vigilante group looking for him.

Red ducked behind his paper as he asked the question.

"When working on a team," said Red.

"Excuse me," said a Mr. Sterling.

"I can't hear you, could you please repeat what you ..."

Red pulled the paper down just below his nose as the vigilantes spread out over the office.

"The dog is outside," Red heard someone say.

"He's in here."

Red hissed at a Mr. Sterling.

"I said, when you work as a member of a *fucking* team, what role do you usually take?

"Can you hear me now?"

A Mr. Sterling sat straight, gripped his briefcase handle and moved his lips, though Red did not hear.

Before a Mr. Sterling stopped, Red scooted up closer, his knees touching a Mr. Sterling's knees. A Mr. Sterling pushed back into his own chair as far as he could.

Red White looked at the next person in line, a fat woman in a tank top. He showed her his tongue and she stepped back one half step, keeping her eyes on Red.

Red White then faced off again with a Mr. Sterling.

"Do you believe Oswald killed Kennedy?" he asked.

A Mr. Sterling said something, but Red White was not interested in any answers.

"Do you even know about The Matrix?" he said.

"And you still choose not to understand?

"Why I oughta ..."

Red White unclenched his fist, took a deep breath and let the blood go out of his face for a moment.

"Do you believe there is such a thing as working too hard?

"Have you ever in your entire life, went a whole day without smiling?"

A Mr. Sterling was now looking for a way out, but was crammed into the small space by Red White's scuffed knees.

"People like to find money," said Red White.

"Are you prepared, in your next job, if you ever get one, that is, if we decide to let you live, to leave money on the sidewalk. ... People like to find money. Well, a Mr. Sterling? Are you willing to drop some of your money in certain assigned public spaces to make people happy if it is required for your employment?"

A Mr. Sterling nodded.

"Lies are all we have going for us in The United States Of America. Are you willing to be a part of this lie?"

Again a Mr. Sterling nodded.

Red White pushed back, giving a Mr. Sterling some scant space.

A Mr. Sterling seemed to relax, but stiffened again when Red appeared to find the killer, crusher life-changing question on the job interview sheet.

"One last question," Red White said, making mega direct eye-contact and showing a lot of sincerity and energy and American can-do.

"Do you believe in talking dogs?" said Red.

"There he is!" shouted one of the vigilantes.

Red White put his hands up and closed his eyes, took a quick deep breath, awaiting the coup de grace.

He heard shuffling and scuffling as the vigilantes wrestled someone to the ground out on the sidewalk.

He opened his eyes, saw that a Mr. Sterling was gone, nodded to the fat woman in the tank top to come on over, then saw that Blue was on the sidewalk with a young man squatted next to him, petting him with a hand holding a cellphone. Blue glared in through the window, nodding repeatedly that it was time to leave Dodge.

"Just sit here for as long as you can," Red White said to the woman.

"Until you have to poop. Please collect that poop and bring it back to us in a plastic Walmart bag. We have to, since 9/11. Trust me. It's necessary."

The woman nodded.

"Umm." Red White was not really wanting to leave his position of power.

"I also have some questions."

He knew, he knew that Blue was impatient to be going, but still, and maybe he could help this fat woman in pink find a cleaning job for eight dollars and save her life for six months or so.

He searched the desk top for answers and felt the man in blue standing right behind him.

"He's right behind me, isn't he?" Red White asked the woman.

She nodded.

Red White looked down, the outlaw finally captured.

Okay, you got me, Red thought.

He looked right down at a piece of paper that had his name on top in official type and font.

It had the marks for the questions Red had answered and at the bottom ... the man in blue's recommendations.

The man in blue cleared his throat in a manner that was meant to be loudly, but was not really that loud.

Red White read as fast as he could.

He scanned his finger down the page.

It said that Red was being recommended for a job!

Red smiled, shook the fat little woman in pink's hand.

"You don't have to poop," he said in a quick whisper.

"Unless you really, really want to. And then, yes, bring it in."

Red White stood, turned and shook the hand of the man with the blue shirt, blue tie and tomato sauce stain, plowed right through the jittery crowd, the glass double doors and ran down the street because he finally, in his whole life, knew where he was going.

Blue followed, ears flapping, feeling the breeze on his wet nose and fur, happy to be moving.

"Woof!

"Woof!"

Chapter THIRTEEN

Red White slammed on the brakes and careened into The Purple People Plasma Center.

At the front desk he asked how to get signed up.

They gave him a folder to read and a video to watch and asked if Blue wished to join him.

The plasma workers asked Red a host of questions.

They weighed him, took his blood pressure, made sure he and Blue had eaten a good meal that morning, which they had not, but Red said they had in order to expedite matters pertaining to his new position.

He wanted to get going.

A worker wearing a clear plastic face shield and green scrubs with the smiling alien with two antenna's in his head Purple People Plasma cartoon logo mascot led Red White and Blue to a big open room filled with rows of reclining bed-like hard blue benches.

There were TVs on the walls and the hard bed-like blue benches were filled with people lying there with needles and tubes stuck into their arms.

The worker gave Red and Blue adjoining hard blue bed benches.

As the worker rubbed his arm with an alcohol swab and told him to clench his fist, Red White looked around, all swelled up like a new minister in a new church, new town, nobody knows me.

He looked at all the fat people, attendants, nurses, TVs, old magazines.

They did not seem to notice him or they were waiting for the right time, circumstance to introduce themselves, when they were not connected to the machines.

Red stretched out, crossed his legs, grabbed an old magazine, peeked over the top of the magazine at the game show on the TV high on the wall.

He couldn't quite see the screen as it was down the line a bit, but heard the people screaming and smiled.

The person across the aisle from Red White stared at the TV across from her, somewhere up high behind Red. Because of the tubes it was only possible to stare at the TVs on the opposite side.

She lounged on the hard cushions like a tart, harlot, strumpet, fille de joie in biblical times, as if she had been here a thousand and one times and would be a thousand more.

She wore pajama bottoms with a certain pattern and a Purple People Plasma T-shirt that Red White knew from his orientation that he would be eligible for a drawing after his first twenty visits.

She wore sandals or flip-flops or thongs and alternated between playing some sort of enjoyable game on her phone and looking up and smiling, sometimes guffawing, in danger of throwing up, at the television.

Red pushed himself up to sit straight in order to see over his personal machine. He tried not to see how his red blood had filled the clear tube and seemed to be shushing back and forth like a washing machine.

He saw Blue lying in his own bed, curled up, trying to cover himself with his ears and tail, eyes closed, attached to his own machine.

Red lay back, rested his free arm behind his head, careful not to close his eyes. The attendants like to know that everyone is okay.

"So don't close your eyes, okay?"

"Okay."

He pumped his tubed hand when the wrap on his arms constricted as he had been instructed in order to encourage the plasma, platelets, antigoblins, blood cell taking and refurbishing process.

With his tube full of blood, his chest filled with fire, with hope, with pride: position, money, community standing.

A debit card.

He closed his eyes for a quick nap and received promptly a reassuring blue hand on his shoulder. He looked up into the clear face shield and the alien Purple People Plasma cartoon character logo and the inquiring eyes and vowed to himself and to the worker and the world that he would not sleep on the job.

Down the line, above the low-key hum of the workers checking on their patients and the televisions, Red heard a man talking to someone across the aisle, telling about his recent bout with congestive heart failure.

"It sounds bad, right?"

And the person on the other side has no choice but to nod and to try to pay attention while keeping one eye on their game show.

"It is and it ain't."

And the man went on for thirty minutes.

Red had no choice but to time him on the big clock because from where he sat he saw the woman in pattern pajamas, the door to an empty office and the big clock.

The man told about feeling ill, then a bit better and then ill again, his trip into the hospital, inside the hospital, interactions with family members, the diagnostic process, life inside a hospital, getting out of the sick room into the lobby, the elevator, the release, the short wheelchair ride and getting into the car on the curb.

All the while shouting at the man across the way, in parts nodding and sneaking a peak at *The Price Is Right.*

Red's eyes popped open like busted shades and he sat straight up as far as the red tube would allow him when he heard voices.

The big, white-tiled, yellow-walled plasma room began to fill with large men led by the head nurse in her white nurse's cap and also by a thick, balding, older man in a too-large suit, the CEO of Purple People Plasma.

Red waved his free hand as he felt a certain connection since the man had been featured on Red's orientation video presentation just minutes ago.

The nurse and Red's nascent friend led The Tuesday Noon Kiwanis Sertoma Jaycees Legion Moose Tour through the facility.

They shook hands with the people on the hard blue bed benches, stopped to watch the TVs and comment on the good reception.

They talked to the blood worker attendants and tried on the face shields, perused the needles and ammonia swabs, the red clear tubes, the magazines.

The group stopped for a while at Blue's bench.

One of the Moose thought of petting Blue then had a second thought.

The big tour group completed its lap around the big room in eight minutes.

Red timed them. He had no choice.

They all stopped as a large group at the end of Red's blue bench bed.

Red watched them.

The nurse said a few words.

Red timed her.

Then someone from the Jaycees asked a question.

Red timed the question and response.

And then the CEO raised his hand and said something about how the blood plasma being collected today would go to soldiers overseas.

"This allotment will go to troops overseas, keeping us free, fighting terrorism," the CEO said.

All the Kiwanis, Sertoma, Jaycees, Legion club members and the one

Moose clapped.

Red White sensed Blue's one eye now open.

Red White thought about the red debit card he would soon be getting, the hope, the pride, position, money, community standing.

He looked over at Blue and they both knew.

Red began to shiver as his machine was now completing the cycle, sending back room-temperature platelets, glutens, goblins and ant bodies to his arm.

Blue pushed himself up to stand in his blue bed bench.

Red stood in his.

He towered over the tour group, could see the whole room, all the TVs, clocks, red tubes, machines.

Red took a deep breath as he gazed at the display about the T-shirt drawing and one of the workers came over to ask if he was feeling okay.

He raised a clenched fist high in the air, the arm connected to the machine.

He felt a sting and a burn and a pull because of the needle and the tape on the hair.

His tube became disconnected like a runaway car wash hose.

Blood spurted from the tiny hole in the vein in his left arm and from the tube.

Blue gave a yelp and a howl as he tugged free and leaped to the floor feet outstretched like Rin Tin Tin or somebody.

The workers with the face shields rushed over.

Their face shields became spotted red. They slid on the tile floor, and at least one fell down on the slick white tile, on his stomach, arms outstretched.

Red's blood hose flopped around and sprayed the tour group like kids in the backyard and Uncle Randy from upstairs with the garden hose again, their suits, their faces, their shoes, the white nurse's cap and somehow only the top of the CEO's balding head, not his baggy suit.

"We live on lies!"

Red White shouted from the blue bench bed as if it were Mount Sinai, with a fountain of blood spurting from behind him.

He pointed an accusing finger at a man in a Kiwanis club blazer.

"I wish I had a harmonica!" shouted Red.

Red pointed both hands, both pointer fingers at the scurrying rats of the service clubs.

"People like to find money," said Red.

"It makes them happy," he said as he was gripped by two attendants by the elbows and eased down from the hard bed.

And as he was being hustled away he saw the young man with the cellphone talking to the front desk woman.

Chapter FOURTEEN

R ed White opened his eyes.
His hands were pressed flat under his head for a pillow.

His knees crunched to his stomach.

He blinked his eyes, twice, to get the sleepy blurry out of them.

The sun was already so bright, way high up, climbing, getting better by the moment, over the buildings and trees and water tower, sitting perfect as a Christmas angel atop the grain elevator, balancing on one sharp point, just for a moment.

He saw something, a being in its craft, its vehicle, its vessel.

He smelled donuts as the breeze shifted and he heard people waking up, moving, starting cars, talking, planning, figuring stuff out once again.

It wore a cap of some sort.

And it blinked back at him.

Or not.

Interesting.

Red White blinked, blinked.

Maybe he was doing Morse Code, he didn't know, but maybe he was, and he could communicate with the creature in the cap in the window of the ship.

He blinked again, reached for his glasses and saw that he was staring right into the eyes of a police man.

Red White sat up on the bench and looked at the time on the big clock on top of the old bank on the four-way that was now a pizza joint.

Red kept staring at the police man and tried to remember his dream.

He felt Blue at his feet. He slid his toes under Blue's stomach, all warm and soft and furry, like slippers.

His dream was quickly slipping away, but he could still remember something, about food, maybe, a certain type of food, or trees, one or many, or weather maybe.

Red stared at the police man, trying not to blink.

Red was tired of the police.

He was tired of lots of things, he decided.

Maybe he decided in the dream about food, certain food, and trees and weather.

Maybe.

He shoved his hand into his pocket, not caring that the police man across the street was staring at him. He touched the note from the waitress.

Still there.

The Matrix.

The cocksucking Matrix.

The bastards.

Oh, well, thought Red White, wiggling his toes inside his shoes under his soft slippers.

He looked around on the cement for a harmonica and for money, then stared right back at the police man.

We live on lies, Diet Pepsi and muffins.

There is nothing else.

The thought boiled inside Red.

He had to tell someone.

The Great Man Philosophy.

Things get done because some body decides to do it.

It makes sense, thought Red White.

He wished someone would do something and had a thought.

He pulled his feet out from under Blue's stomach, stood and stretched his arms and yawned.

He shivered, as he did every morning before coffee and walked straight across the street toward the staring, unblinking police man in the black and white police car.

Red White stalked across the street, big steps.

Blue opened one eye to watch while the other eye slept on.

Red began to boil.

He was just so angry at so many things, and this police man was going to get an earful. And they could send him to jail.

What-ever.

Red opened his mouth to shout and then stopped walking, stopped his talking.

He shook his head.

Blue closed his eye.

Red touched the police car and the mannequin kept staring at his stomach.

It was a fake police man with black plastic hair and even a mole, inside a real police car to get people to not speed right through town, Red surmised.

And someone had turned the head to stare at Red.

So funny.

Maybe the waitress had not meant the note for Red that day.

Maybe she had dropped it.

Maybe she looked for it the rest of the day after Red had left with his family determined to change everything.

It was meant for someone else.

He wasn't even supposed to be here.

He turned and walked back to Blue, not checking for traffic, not wondering if it would rain, not feeling hungry or thirsty, not caring if the trees would be beautiful this fall.

Not a fucking thing.

Chapter FIFTEEN

And so, what would he do, after doubting himself so severely, his mission, his path.

What would anyone do.

What should you do.

What could you do.

Do you have options or does it just not matter, plop down on a piece of ice and let yourself drift off to the middle of city park pond.

Hmmm.

Well, for a while Red White and Blue moped around town. Blue's ears moped and Red's arms moped.

They sat on every bench at the city park, sat alone in the third-base bleachers at the Legion ball field.

They sat in the lawn furniture display in the parking lot at Walmart and they sat in a portable duck blind at the gun store on Fourth Street.

They sat in the window booth at the café on South Street, sipping water, watching people on the street, twirling the water glass in between their hands and front paws, staring, thinking.

Red was thinking and Blue could tell.

Blue was thinking and Red kinda figured.

On the way up the long metal steps to the top of the ol' water tower, with the swear words on top, about halfway up, Red paused, looked down at Blue trying to make his way, get his four legs all in rhythm and working together.

Red looked straight up.

Far enough.

And he looked straight out and all around while hearing Blue's toenails clanking on the hard, sharp metal, and Blue's whining.

50

Red White looked out across his town.

He saw his house where he was a kid and over there he saw his house where he was a man, and the alley that ran between.

He saw the church and the café right there and the other one over there kind of behind that tree.

There's the old gas station.

The ball field. The movie house, where they saw "Our Town," and "It's A Wonderful Life," "101 Dalmatians," all that shit. All those people, the school, and kids on the playground like happy ants.

He moved his arms around and scooted his feet, slowly, so he could stand facing the town like a swimmer on the high dive, the very top.

And the lifeguards don't even see you. They're doing other stuff. And your Mom and Dad are eating at the stand with your brother and sister and your friends are timing each other for how long they can stay under.

And there is no one to watch you.

Red White held on to the sharp, hard, metal ladder with his hands backward.

He felt the hard, ridged metal on his fingers.

He moved his feet without looking, slide, slide, to the side, back again.

Red saw the smoke.

Perfect smoke curling above the trees, then heard the first toots of the horn as the train wound around the curve of the lake's edge.

Red looked down and saw Blue's mouth open wide and the terror in his eyes as he fought to climb the thin, sharp metal steps of the water tower.

Blue howled along with the train as it hit the crossing in the middle of town.

Red pushed one foot off his step to start down as Blue lost his balance.

He stumbled and fell, smacking his jaw on a step.

Blue yelped and tried to run. His ears flapped in the air.

Red shuddered at the thump of the soft brown body on the hard, unforgiving ground.

Blue lay there, stretched out, silent.

Red White took one step into the air, stretched his foot and decided he could not get there quick enough.

He pushed off with his hands.

One foot caught a step and tossed him end over end.

"Ooomph!"

Red landed on his back, harder than he thought possible.

In an instant he understood how high up he had been.

A fish fighting for life, he stretched his mouth wide and reached out both arms, patting the ground wildly, a blind man after the quarter, looking for Blue.

Red White found Blue with the tips of his fingers, felt the soft, brown fur, stared up at the white, fluffy sky, and drifted to sleep like a floating ball lost at sea, to the sound of the train in the distance, the rolling hum of a hundred cars and the goodbye of the toots, a white stream from an airplane, knowing help was on the way.

Red's eyes just opened.

He did not open them.

They opened on their own.

Because Red was sleeping, knocked-out, tired, dog-tired.

He would have rather just ...

He sat straight up.

There was Blue. His back.

Red White crawled to Blue, shoved his nose and his wet eyes into the dog's brown fur.

Red sobbed, cursed himself, tasted the brown fur on his tongue. He kicked the ground hard with his toes, trying to commit injury.

Blue moaned.

Red leaped over Blue, took the dog's head in his hands and kissed his furry cheeks, his head.

Red looked deep into Blue's hung-over eyes.

He shot to his feet and stuck both fists into the sky.

He punched the sky, left, right, left, and he did an actual somersault.

Blue lay across Red White's knees.

Red's back rested against one of the legs of the ol' water tower with the swear words on top.

A grey squirrel hopped around, not seeming to see them.

It hopped, hopped, sniffed the sir, sat still.

What in God's name could it be wondering about, as it decided to hop, hop, sit still, think deeply, hop once more, with a purpose.

Blue also watched the squirrel and tired of the charade.

Blue growled and the squirrel ran away like the church was on fire.

"Yes, ol' Blue," said Red White.

"Squirrels are such linear thinkers."

Blue wagged his tail, watching the little animal disappear in the weeds and little trees.

"But what are you gonna do?"

Red grabbed an acorn and tossed it with his wrong hand at a post.

"They're squirrels, huh?"

Just then the young man with the cell phone huffed and puffed as he walked up the hill.

The young man sat on the grass. He wore white shirt and black pants, black shoes.

He petted Blue and held out the phone to Red White.

"You have a message," he said.

"It's not my phone," said Red.

"You have a message," said the young man.

Red said he didn't know how to work the phone, so the young man worked it for him and again held it out for Red.

Red took it and read the message.

"Hello, son. You are doing good. I am proud of you."

Red read out loud.

"How do you know it's for me?" he asked the young man.

The young man stood, brushed himself off and said he didn't really.

"You just look like you could use some good news. Maybe that's it.

"Well, seeya," he said, and he walked back down the hill.

Red White and Blue watched him go.

"Well, that was weird," said Red.

Blue nodded.

"But I'll take it."

Red ran his hand down Blue's back and took comfort in the low rumble in Blue's throat.

Blue ran his paws through a crop of clover.

And sure enough, there it was, a four-leaf.

Red thought to pick it and he just touched it, took a mental photo.

Red thought about going down and seeing what the guys were talking about at coffee today.

Red took a stick and could not resist poking a big, round ant hill to see all the little black ants suddenly scurrying around, trying to make things right, as they were, perfect.

Red thought about going back to pursue his plasma career.

Red thought about checking them both into the hospital for checkups after their nasty tumbles and being fed in bed.

And decided in silence ... naaaah.

"But I'll tell ya what we *will* do."

He said out loud as he checked Blue's ears and fur for ticks and his own head for bumps.

Chapter SIXTEEN

Blue went first because he had a pretty good idea where they were headed.

Blue stood at the door, the glass door of The Quik Stop.

Red White walked in and Blue followed him right to the markers.

Blue watched Red looking at them.

Red pointed.

Blue snatched the black marker in his mouth.

He trotted along, wagging his tail as Red walked out of the store.

Red smiled and chatted quickly with the workers.

"Oh, what a cute dog," they smiled.

"I wish I had one."

"Have a nice day."

"You too."

They stopped on the edge of the parking lot for Red to fetch the wet marker from Blue's mouth.

He wiped it on his pants.

CHAPTER SEVENTEEN

Blue lay in the soft, green, freshly cut lawn, in the sun on Maple Street. Red White knelt in the grass, fiddling with the For Sale sign.

Red unscrewed and pulled out and somehow got the sign out of the metal holder.

He scrambled, on his knees, holding the sign in front of him with both hands to set it flat on the driveway.

Blue stayed where he was while Red leaned hard over the sign, working.

Red White crawled back the same way, smiling, admiring his work.

Blue sniffed the air at the pungent black Magic Marker aroma and watched as Red dug in the grass to find the screws again, was distracted by a herd of clover, fitted the sign back into its holder and stepped back to admire his vandalism.

They strolled down the sunny street with their black Magic Marker, stopping at the next For Sale sign.

Red White wanted to say so much, and he had to make the words smaller and smaller as he moved on from sign to sign across town.

Blue tried to find shade where he could but mostly just lay in the sun.

... there's something wrong with the world
... like a splinter in your mind
... to blind you from the truth
... they will fight to protect it

At the end of the day when Red White and Blue had finished their work they dragged up to The Ice Cream Shoppe.

Blue's white stomach was stained green like Red's knees.

Blue grinned and wagged his tail, made his eyes as bright as a newborn pup.

Red smiled and waved even before he got to the tiny window.

He leaned down to see eye to eye with the girl in the little square hole inside which she controlled access to the ice cream, within reach of the sprinkles and the chocolate dip and the twist machine.

Oh what a cute little doggie.
He's so hungry and thirsty.
99 cents.
Water?
I can give you water.
Do you have any left over ice cream you were going to throw away.
No, we don't throw any away.
Oh.
Don't you have any money?
No. He doesn't have any money.
The dog can talk!
Oh, yeah. All dogs talk, don't they?
No! No dogs talk!
Say something, something else.
He talks for ice cream.
Okay. Okay.
What do you want?

The dog and the old man sat at the little picnic table with sprinkles, dip cones, twist cones, cherry-vanilla cones.

Blue lapped up water out of a little rainbow cup.

Then they swang on the swings in the park.

They took turns pushing each other and then leaped off together, astronauts landing on Mars, having to jump out of their space ships because they were out of gas!

Oh, my!

They went to the café and after a few hours each of the napkins in the six holder machines had messages for the people.

They walked down main street, moseying, pausing to look for cops and writing on the front windows of every single shop when nobody was looking.

They paused at the end of the street to look back, admiring their work, feeling good about themselves because that was fun.

Blue took off across the street, not looking, his ears blowing and his tail wagging.

"Hey!" Red shouted, running at a limp, after ol' Blue, looking both ways and behind him, and not seeing any cars either parked or moving.

"Blue! Be careful!"

CHAPTER EIGHTEEN

The full spectrum dominance Bluetooth four-quad Bose stereo speaker MarsBox Radio played loud, announcing Mr. and Mrs. Scott and Suzie Scott as they pulled hard into the driveway in their new blaze orange Command Sub Shark SUV, for which they had gotten a good deal from local dealer Hjal Hjaallssoonnhh.

Right away Suzie saw the sign.

The For Sale sign.

"What the?" she said as she began to hop out her side even before Scott stopped.

She stormed to the sign, then stomped back to confront Scott as he as he got out, leaving his door open and the radio playing, and with a quizzical look on his face picked up the paper on the front step.

"What is that supposed to mean!"

Her face was red and her arms were pointing.

Scott said he did not understand.

He began to understand more when Suzie kicked him in the knee, ripped the newspaper from his hands and tore it up in front of him, stomped into the house crying, locked the door, knocked out the big front picture window and began firing at Scott with the 30.06.

He ducked and crawled under the Sub Shark while the full spectrum Bose, four-quad remained on full blast, playing to the neighborhood and over the town.

> I see trees of green,
> red roses too.
> I see them bloom,

for me and you.
And I think to myself,
what a wonderful world.

At The Café, the Rogers family sat in their favorite window booth. Each had a big menu. They smiled across the table at each other, the children and the mom and dad. They watched the people go by outside and they smiled at the people they knew at the other tables.

The Dad greeted the waitress as she stopped to ask them what she could get for them today.

Little Jeffrey-Michael grabbed a napkin from the holder to have something to do until it was his turn.

He spread it out in front of him and put a finger on each word as he read to himself with his lips.

His sister across from him shooshed him even though he wasn't making much of a sound. She grabbed her own napkin to *show* him and she began reading.

Then all the kids wanted napkins with the funny words and the waitress and Mom & Dad had some trouble getting each of them to pay attention to ordering and to what was going on here.

Dad asked to have the napkin holder passed to him.

He set it down firmly in front of him so it would not be a distraction.

The waitress, wanting to see what had become of the napkins that she herself was in charge of, took out a napkin and read the words, out loud, which Dad thought inappropriate in a family restaurant and grabbed the wife's arm. She grabbed the next child and they all grabbed each other and left the restaurant like a conga line caterpillar, out the door, down the walk and into the sedan.

Inside the car, Dad hit Mom, she slapped the closest kid across the mouth with the back of her hand, the kids thumped each other in the heads with their fists.

Dad fought off Mom as he pulled into the street and ran the sedan head-first into a garbage truck just getting up to speed and headed for the high school.

I see skies of blue,
And clouds of white.
The bright blessed day,
The dark sacred night.

And I think to myself,
What a wonderful world.

Mr. Palmer pulled his car up to the front curb. He stopped, as he always did, right there. He got out and proceeded to make his way into Mr. Myers' Hardware Store.

He stopped right as he was putting a nickel into the parking meter because fifteen minutes was all he would need, today or any other day.

He looked and cocked his head at the curious writing on Myers' front window announcing today's specials, placing his hands on his hips and tilting his head this way and that to try to figure it all out.

Mr. Myers came out to ask Mr. Anderson what was the matter, why didn't he just come on in?

Mr. Palmer pointed and together they twisted and turned and squinted and stepped forward then back to the curb, then even farther back, into the street, then forward again.

Together they moved, synchronized movers who had practiced for days maybe.

Then Mr. Myers realized.

He turned and threw a fist at Mr. Palmer's temple and knocked him flat to the street.

Mr. Meyers kicked Mr. Palmer in the buttocks.

He unzipped his pants and peed on Mr. Palmer still lying in the street, cars going by, people beginning to appear in doors and windows.

The colors of the rainbow,
So pretty in the sky.
Are also on the faces,
Of people going by,
I see friends shaking hands.
Saying, "How do you do?"
They're really saying,
"I love you".

People stood on the cement bridge walkway and pointed across the river at the writing on the old railway ties stuck in the middle of the stream.

Some kids stopped their bikes to read the new words on the underside of the bridge.

Motorists stopped too long at intersections to read everything that was now on some of the stop signs.

At the post office, just underneath the little slot, a three by five card was taped which made Mrs. Francis shake her head and tsk-tsk.

In the teachers meeting after school wads of paper and spit balls fired back and forth every time the principal turned her back.

The ministers at the golf club, having their afternoon fellowship out on the patio drew looks from The Ladies Wednesday Afternoon League along with hisses of "wankjob, peckerhead, testes twirler, twatwaffle, motherfucker, cocksucker, dickweed, dickbag, douchewaffle, lard-ass, dick juice, gaytard, fuktard, fuckbrain, fuknut, fuckface and fukwad."

> I hear babies cry,
> I watch them grow,
> They'll learn much more,
> Than I'll ever know.
> And I think to myself,
> What a wonderful world.

The folks working in The Big Store in the aisles and at the cash registers and in the expanded complaint department with a lounge and happy hour heard everything from their neighbors who had been outside.

And everyone knew who had did it.

Everything used to be okay.

The waiting lines at the checkout, which used to be nine miles long were now ten miles long because everyone was talking.

Their faces were red and their arms were waving and pointing this way and that.

They knew who did it.

They knew just who.

> Yes, I think to myself,
> What a wonderful world.

The department supervisors of The Big Store made their workers go get the pitchforks. They put in *NOW!* orders for more pitchforks.

They found the barbecue tongs still in the boxes and the big knives and the sharp knives.

The department supervisors yelled at their workers and the workers got the tomatoes and the tar and the matches and the charcoal and wiener roasters and the rope.

They got the guns.

And the bullets.

Oh yeah.

Chapter NINETEEN

Red White followed Blue down the sidewalk, working hard to keep the ol' dog in sight.

Then Red stopped, stood up straight and understood.

He saw where Blue was headed and he smiled, wiped the sweat from his brow.

Red sat down next to Blue on the front porch of the old filling station.

There were the old chairs and some holes in the floor, cracked steps, lots of dust.

The signs were all stolen or blown away. Birds sat in the bullet holes in the windows staring at Red White and Blue like who do you guys think you are.

One of the old red pumps sat off to the side in the weeds and old tires.

Blue's ears popped.

He had an idea, it seemed.

He pushed open the old door with his nose and trotted on in.

Red White could hear Blue inside nosing around.

Something fell and Red almost got up to go see when he saw Blue coming out, his ears all proud and shit.

He set it on the wood by Red.

Red smiled wide, patted Blue's head.

"Oh, Blue, you found it."

Red rubbed it on his pants and patted the back to make the years fall out the holes.

He put it in his mouth and it fit so perfect.

He played a tune, squeaky and then a little better.

Blue moaned, settled in and closed his eyes.

They heard slamming of doors and shouting down the street as Red played.

He crossed his legs and leaned back against the old porch pillar.

Then one of Blue's ears went up.

He jumped up and went back inside.

Red played low on the harp and up high and in the middle. He drew and he blew and he cupped his hands and did all the stuff he could remember and then he did them again.

Blue set down the old Folgers can right next to Red.

Red looked at it and kept playing.

Blue nosed away some of the cobwebs and Red saw money in there, old dusty bills and change.

"Well, Blue, put it on out there," said Red as he continued to play.

So Blue carried the can in his teeth out into the street and feathered the change and the bills around.

Some kids came by.

And some old people.

And a waitress on her way home, walking.

They found the money, looking with their eyes at Red and Blue to say whose is this and did I just find money?

Red kept playing and didn't look and Blue was asleep anyway so they could just have the money, and they smiled.

At the TV station it was almost time for The News.

The man went outside for a smoke while the woman went to the restroom.

The man stood by the building, on the sidewalk, puffing.

He saw his car over there next to the woman's car.

He saw in his back window some writing and he stalked over there to take a look.

He read it, fired the cigarette butt at the cement, turned and stalked back into the station.

The newscasters and news team got ready for the show as they did every day. The anchors snuggled into their desk seats as someone helped them with their microphones and one last hair touch-up.

They stared hard at the Teleprompter.

CLAIRE:

"And now, tonight, the last in our series of Local Heroes/Our Warriors.

"The Great Man philosophy of how things change."
STU:
The great ideas come from great heroes.
CLAIRE:
"Today, National Guard Commandant Buckley Buckholtz, Jr."
Stu, the man, listened as she did her special and then said, "And that's about it for us, have a good weekend, and ..."
Claire cut in.
"And no word lately on that one gentlemen, what was his name?"
"Oh, yes, him ... well ... actually ...," said Stu.

Red White heard the people coming.
The feet on hard-scrabble soil, the pitchforks twanging when they bumped together.

He kept playing and Blue kept sleeping as the old people and the kids and the waitress stood around listening, longer than they really had time for.

The police cars pulled up, one, two, three, then three more and two more and then one, with lights flashing, bouncing off the old wood.

Then the TV SUV pulled up and the crew piled out, big lights shining.

Blue awakened, got up and hopped down the little bit off the old sagging porch. He stretched and yawned and barked.

He walked out more, closer, as the people and the pitchforks and the knives became shadows in between the police cars and the night and the flashing lights.

A tomato hit behind Blue on the wall and another smacked him in the head.

Blue barked.

And then.

Everything grew quiet.

Everyone watched Red White as the last of the crowd pulled up, shoving in, pushing the people in front up farther than they wanted to be.

Red White pulled the harmonica down from his mouth.

He rubbed it on his pants.

Blue moved out closer, toward the crowd and the police.

While Blue stalked closer to the lynch mob, Red blew into the three hole and drew to check that everything was still working.

"What did you say!" shouted a police captain on a bullhorn looking right at Blue.

And then three or four policemen raised their rifles and so did some of the men in the crowd.

Red White heard clicking of hammers and looked up.

He jumped and ran toward them all, toward Blue.

"No!

"No!"

He shouted, his arms reaching out farther and faster than his legs could run.

"I said it!

"I said it!"

"Boom!

"Boom-boom!

"Boom!"

"Boom.

"Pop."

"Twanggg."

The ground ran red for a moment like a flash-flood tomato soup river.

The air filled with smoke and pitchforks.

Red reached and dived and then stood up straight.

All around him were bullet holes, pockmarks, and pitchforks, some few tomato spots and seeds in the dust.

Blue stood in the middle, one leg outstretched, one claw just touching the ground. He was bent in the middle and held it. His head was twisted and his jaw open as if he had barely escaped a bullet.

He held the pose.

His big eyes searched to see who was watching. His tail was straight up and one leg up like he was using the fire hydrant.

Red looked at it all, the people froze in stop-action, their wide eyes, as if he were stepping into a painting.

He reached and touched the four-leaf clover on Blue's collar that must have attached itself while Blue was rolling in the grass.

The only motion in the whole setting was something on the ground, a line, a spreading mass, retreating, flowing back.

Red eased to one knee and leaned low to see the ants from a hill that had been struck by one of the bullets, scattering, frantic, moving every possible way and back again.

He saw familiar feet.

He looked up into the eyes of his wife and children.

They smiled and hugged him and kissed him.

A tear fell down Red's cheek.

Behind them stood the waitress.

She looked as if she had something to say.

Red's wife stepped back to see Red exchanging looks with the waitress.

She began to cry, gathered her now grown children in her arms and began herding them away.

"Always the waitress, Red!

"Always the waitress!

"Never the wife."

The waitress had something in her hand.

Red reached out to take it.

It was Red's harmonica, lost in the commotion.

She turned and left, melting into the crowd and the dark.

"It's not the same one!"

Red shouted into the dark.

"Different waitress!"

"So."

"That dog can really talk?"

"Really?"

The people gathered around Red and Blue and the pitchforks.

"Umm, yeah," said Red.

"I mean, no. No. He can't. Actually, that's just ..."

"No, man!"

Someone ran up and pointed at Blue.

"We saw it!

"That dog right there talked, plain as day while you was way over there!"

And they all cheered, raised Red White and Blue up on their shoulders, turned on the lights and the sirens again and had a parade through town, down main street, to the ice cream store.

Waitresses sat on Red's knees while he ate his chocolate dip.

Blue sat at another table, surrounded by city dignitaries and the like.

The next week Red White and Blue perched at the news desk between Claire and Stu.

And for the first time in a very long time Red White felt plugged in, a part of things, in the main stream, swimming with the guys.

During Homecoming Week all the store windows, all the cars and all the homes sported quotes from *The Waitress Matrix.*

The high school musical was *The Waitress Matrix* that year.

In the café nobody talked about TV shows. They all talked about favorite scenes from the previews of *The Waitress Matrix II.*

The same with family discussions during dinner and in the teacher's lounge.

The high school repeated the same play in the spring and the high school debate team took second place in regionals.

The town signs at the edge of town changed.

"The Red Pill Town."

... choosing to be one who understands, not one who chooses to remain in la-la land.

With an inset picture of "Blue The Talking Dog."

And, later that same year, on a bright sunny summer morning, Red White climbed the water tower with Blue wrapped over his shoulders.

They inched up and up.

They made it to the top, all the way to the swear words.

Red White turned around, carefully, to face the town, the picture perfect town.

He held Blue in his arms.

He pushed off.

And away they flew.

For a few seconds they flew.

And then they smacked into one of the big hot air balloons set up in the big open space under the water tower for the big celebration set up to honor the local talking dog.

They hit hard.

Both had the air knocked out of them and they sucked breath as they slid down the side of the big orange-orange balloon, landing feet-first on the ground, as no one noticed.

Red let Blue down and Blue gave him a look.

Red moaned, discouraged, not knowing who he was or what to do.

He had hoped the big suicide scene would seal his legendary fate that people would remember forever.

He would be the hero of his wife and his children and the one waitress from a long time ago if she wasn't in a nursing home and couldn't hear the TV, and maybe that other waitress from that one night.

And now that everyone knew The Waitress Matrix script, word for word, what was there left for him to do.

Not too much.

A talking dog, revolution and then where do you go?

It was still the same town, just that everyone knew about "The Waitress Matrix."

It hadn't made that much of a difference.

Blue was a big celebrity.

They thought he could talk.

Maybe he could.

Red wasn't that interested.

He sighed and remembered that wonderful night when they were on the run, had money to spread out, and made people happy, and he played the harmonica, and even though it drew sporadic small arms fire it had not sounded that bad.

He sat again against the water tower as Blue nosed all around.

In a few seconds he remembered all his life, as a child, student, husband, father, working father, father in the restaurant, father on the street, guy on the street.

And how he had found Blue.

On that one day.

Out in front of the movie theater, the turn of the century, Y2K, everything is going to end, we are all going to die, the snow will be so deep.

Make snowshoes, to survive.

You just can't imagine.

It will be difficult.

It will be scary.

But it might be really cool, too.

Purple snow?

Blue was lying there in front of the movie theater showing The Matrix in 1999 as if he had just seen it, and could go no further, or as if he would like to see it.

Red was stumbling along, clutching the note from the waitress in his hand, which someone probably told him were words from "The Logical Song," whatever that was.

Red sat on the street curb and looked into Blue's eyes.

We're done.

Blue seemed to be saying.

We didn't change anything. People are still slaves even though they know they are slaves, or have heard they are slaves. They don't really give a shit.

Nothing changes.

There is nothing more we can do. There is nothing more out there beyond The Logical Song and The Matrix.

That one fat guy movie-maker?

Get serious.

Red White sat on the main street curb next to his dog, crossed his arms, stretched out his feet.

He began to talk but yawned and had to wait to talk.

"Anyway, ya know, I don't really think you're right on this one.

"I still think there is hope in the rolls.

"If there is any hope, it lies in the rolls, buried deep, deep inside those mooshy rolls of fat."

Red White grabbed the one parking meter and pulled himself up.

"Let's go, Blue.

"We've still got work to do.

"No rest for the wicked."

Chapter TWENTY

"Welcome to the store.
"Thank you for coming."
Red White stood near the entrance.
"Hello.
"Good morning.
"You slaughtered eight million people to gain control of these Cheetos and Strawberry pop."

The people scuffled past, some waddled, some too fat to move hummed by on motorized wheel chairs.

"You are poor for a reason. Somebody wants it that way. And if you become too tired to scrounge they have prisons waiting for you."

Blue sat at Red's feet, his eyes closed, not pretending to talk.

"The war on terror ..."

Red used both hands for air quotes.

"Is a joke and a fake and a lie."

He pointed at three people wearing some sort of clothing camo.

"Your sons and daughters are dead for a lie. They are stupid, pitiful murderers and you are worse. Any welcome home parades should proceed directly to the county courthouse for prosecution."

People began to notice Red and drift back toward the entrance from Home Supplies, from Paper, from Checkout.

Red held one hand high, holding a full-color ad for the in-store beauty salon.

"Anyone who would like to be buried at sea, here is a coupon, ten percent off."

Two women and two men began pushing their way through the crowd, with hands raised high, toward Red to get the colored paper.

Now the crowd encircled Red White.

The store workers in their uniforms, the people who had been shopping in Clothing and in The Grocery Store, in Sporting Goods, Everywhere, along with the people just coming in the door, stood tight around Red White the greeter, as if having someone say have a good day or welcome to the store was the greatest thing ever.

Nobody talked.

Somebody talked.

She was shooshed into compliance.

Outside the store the flashing colored lights bounced off the front glass doors, the pop machines, the rows of waiting carts.

Police cars, fire trucks, two ambulances and the TV news van jammed in at odd angles around the front doors.

Volunteer members of the Moose, Kiwanis, Sertoma and Jaycees blocked the alley exit.

Blue slowly raised one eye.

He growled and showed one incisor.

Red turned away and searched for something.

The big crowd stayed quiet, leaning this way, that, to see what he was doing.

He seemed to have found it.

He leaned low and lifted the twelve-pack of Diet Pepsi on top of another.

Red White moaned to climb atop the two twelve-packs, shuffled around like he was on the steps of the water tower to face everyone.

He looked into their upturned faces, like fish at Trout Haven, waiting for anyone to throw them a crumb so they may live one more moment to seek another crumb.

They breathed with open mouths.

Red White did not hate at that moment.

He sighed, sucked in breath as if there were no more.

He reached deep into his pockets and found candy. He tossed them at the people and they held their hands up high to catch.

He smelled Blue's damp fur as it had rained a little as they came in.

"My brothers and sisters."

Red tried to talk loud and he could feel Blue rolling his eyes inside his head, but he meant it.

At this moment he meant it.

"We ...

"You ... me ... they ...

"Did not go to the moon.

"It's all fake."

Red White held up his arms and spread them out as wide as he could, not that far.

He saw a young man in back wearing a wrinkled white shirt smile.

A shiver went down his back and his head tingled because he had been able to be the one who let that young man know he was not the only one.

That is why he had been born.

He had been wondering.

A short, stout woman in a dress she had made herself reached up to shake Red's hand.

Glass shattered.

Crash. *Crash.* Crash.

Rumble.

Tear gas canisters smoked and rolled along the tile floor.

The doors crashed down and the barrel of a tank poked through, feeling blindly like an elephant trunk into a circus tent.

Then soldiers in face masks, knee pads, chest protectors, padded gloves and big blue batons rushed in.

Blue, both eyes open, stood up straight to face them as Red, hit by something, stumbled from the twelve-pack podium and cracked his knee and his head on the glass front window of the beauty salon.

Some of the people chugged back into the store, and some in the crowd, coughing, weeping, turned to face the soldiers.

Red White pulled himself up by the partially finished Desenex display.

A thin red line had formed in the middle of his forehead.

"9/11 was no accident!

"The Simpsons forewarned us!

"The Big Lebowski forewarned us!"

The people raised up their open hands.

Red White pulled himself to the top of the two Diet Pepsi twelve packs.

Shots echoed in the super store.

"Yip! Ow! Ow! Ow! Ow!"

Red White heard Blue yelp.

He looked for the dog amid the knees and feet.

He saw Blue rolling on the floor.

A maroon blood pool formed around Blue.

Blue looked firmly up at Red.

The solid, big loyal dog's eyes said, "Go for it."

Red turned into the smoke and the hands and the eyes and the bullets and the noise.

He held out his arms like a high diver.

He bent his knees as far as they would go, pushed off and jumped into the upturned hands and the arms of the crowd.

"Nine ... e-lev-eeennnn ...!" screamed Red, his body stretched to its full extension, as far as he could possibly go, riding along on the hands of the people.

They love me, he whispered to himself.

"9-1-1.

"Coinky-dink?

"Are you fucking kidding me!

"Charge!"

As Red White pointed at the soldiers and police and shouted, the people threw him into the charging mass of camo.

He flew.

For a moment he flew.

With arms outstretched he headed straight for a state trooper in full Multi-Purpose SuperStore-camo uniform.

Red saw himself in the face shield, getting closer.

Too close.

He stared and saw the wide open mouth, eyes.

Again he saw his life before his eyes, not the whole thing.

Just parts as there wasn't much time.

HOMELAND SECURITY
IF YOU SEE SOMETHING, SAY SOMETHING

THE ORDINARY ADVENTURES OF CORD NORTH

by Mike Palecek

Singing this will be the day that I die.
— Don McLean

The mind of an American rules the world.

The President? Warren Buffett? Tiger Woods? Katie Couric? Jon Stewart? The Michelin Man?

No, stupid, it's you.

You are king of the world, god,

superman, King Midas, all that.

It's you.

You are more than just a legend in your own mind.

You are The Man.

And when the CIA through the CIA propaganda machine called Radio Free Europe or the American Free Press tells you the Russians are coming or the criminals are coming or terrorists or the Iranians or Iraqis of Afghans on nuclear-powered blue donkeys or big bees, and you believe it — well, then, Zeke, that's how the world will go.

You are powerful, the most powerful yahoo who has ever lived in the history of living.

And you are an idiot.

And the world is going to burn.

You are not an idiot-on-purpose,

but an idiot none-the-less.

The CIA, the persons in the CIA, are smart.

But they are evil.

The actual Evil Empire.

And they control you.

The most powerful person in the world.

If you were not an idiot they could not do that.

But you are an idiot.

And that's a bummer, man.

That's. A bummer.

— by Unknown, found in the only known cave in north-central South Dakota by Daughters of The American Revolution during smoke break on a Civil War re-enactment weekend, written on Egyptian-type parchment or papyrus or maybe something else

Chapter ONE

And I pray, oh my god do I pray
I pray every single day
For a revolution

— *Four Non-Blondes*

The mind of an American rules the world.

I get that.

I get all that, but ...

Cord North sat in the pickup on the curb waiting for Jimmy Steve.

Cord stopped the radio dial for a moment to hear about how somebody died.

He thought about all kinds of shit.

The shit he had to do today that he wanted to do, the shit he had to do today that he didn't want to do, the shit he had done that he liked thinking about and the shit that he had done that made him sad.

He also thought about the shit coming, in the future.

And it was coming.

He got that.

He remembered being told by his mother, just like in the movie, that if he got a BB gun he would shoot his eye out and then nothing happened on that, but he did almost get appendicitis once when he ate something.

Cord checked his phone, blew his smoke toward the little opening at the top of his window and messed with the radio, trying to find another sports talk station.

The magnetic sign on the pickup said "Your Home Our Home Security

Systmz."

Cord's cousin had done the lettering and yeah, they wanted to be edgy, but that looked like a mistake, and it was.

Now they had a hundred magnetic signs for the cousins, the uncles, aunts, grandchildren, stationary, business cards, and that whole big thing was all just now dying down.

Cord worked his phone to estimate the job, the white two-story on Simmons.

"That's right," he said.

"Seven, nine, five."

"No. No it's not. Shit."

Cord looked at the house and remembered his own home, not so far from here and that one day.

He tuned the radio, sat back, stared out the windshield, blew smoke, looked in the rearview for Jimmy Steve.

"The fuck you mean?"

Cord had said to his mother.

"How can that be?"

Cord's mother had told him there was not such a thing as the Easter Bunny, and while she was there, nailed Santa Claus and Jesus Christ pretty good, too.

"Cord, don't say fuck," she had said.

"Say poop."

And then he had stormed out the back door, slamming the screen door, looking for Jimmy Steve.

He found him peaking in Jenna Storm's window in broad daylight.

"Hey!"

Cord hollered.

Jimmy Steve hissed and waved his hands down like telling the runner to slide.

"Fuck! Shut up!"

Cord hunched over and got up to Jimmy Steve and they both looked in the window at Jenna in her underwear for a while.

As they were walking down the alley Cord said that his mom wanted him to say poop.

"Then say it," said Jimmy Steve.

"Just make her happy."

Cord stopped in the gravel and waited for Jimmy Steve to stop and walk back to him.

"What's fuck?" said Cord.

"Fuck?" said Jimmy Steve.

"I d'know, just fuck I guess."

"But what is it!" said Cord.

And so Cord and Jimmy Steve had discussed fuck in the middle of the alley for a while and determined it had power, power that had diminished with usage and time, albeit just a little, as in defiance of Cord's mom, and cementing a back alley brotherhood, they had found a cousin who knew how to make tattoos with India ink and a needle and had put "fuck" across the four fingers of their hands, Cord his left and Jimmy Steve his right, and named themselves the Fuck Brothers, and then they found out soon enough what the word meant.

Jimmy Steve slammed the door as he got in and began to tune the radio.

"The fuck is that?"

And then just as quickly got out to snatch the piece of paper stuck in one of the wipers, that Cord had not noticed, until now.

"Hey," said Jimmy Steve as he read the note.

"Just hey?"

"Hey," said Jimmy Steve.

Cord shrugged his shoulders and kept doing what he had been doing.

"How's Northern Pooper doing?" said Jimmy Steve.

"Hear anything?" he said.

"Nope."

Jimmy Steve plowed the dial through a world full of static, back and forth, looking for the pigeon news.

"We had it that one time," he said.

Cord and Jimmy Steve had purchased a racing pigeon, a New York City racing pigeon, through a newspaper ad. For one hundred dollars they got a picture of it and got to name it, a schedule of races and the name and address of the trainer, and a coop-cam link to an online video camera attached to the pigeon pen on an Astoria, Queens rooftop.

Today's race was The Five Boroughs Big Swoop Forty Mile Classic and had been threatened by terror, hawk watch due to clear sky conditions.

"You go up yet?"

Jimmy Steve nodded toward the house.

"No, waiting for you. Where you been, man, geez, it's two-thirty. I thought we was starting at two."

"Had some shit to do.

"Hey, cool."

He stopped the radio dial and smiled up at Cord as the solemn announcer spread out the details of how someone had died.

Then Jimmy Steve sat back, slid down a bit, crossed his arms and settled in like the American spy he considered himself, though he had never told Cord.

He didn't know if he should.

Chapter TWO

"Buddy Holly's death to me was a personal tragedy,"
McLean said. "As a child ... I had no idea that nobody
else felt that way much. I mean, I went to school and
mentioned it and they said, 'So what?'"

Cord North and Jimmy Steve crawled out of the pickup and walked up to the house.

They split at the porch, examining the windows, the windows of the next door neighbors, the windows to the basement, and met in back.

"So?" said Jimmy Steve.

"Yeah," said Cord.

"I guess."

While Jimmy Steve went around again to the front door, Cord got the sign out of the pickup and stuck the metal forks into the front lawn: Your Home Our Home Security Systmz.

He joined Jimmy Steve at the front door. Cord rang the doorbell. Jimmy Steve looked in the windows.

Cord knocked on the door, then pounded.

Cord tried the knob and pushed the door.

It swung open. He pushed at it with the toe of his boot.

Jimmy Steve followed Cord inside the darkened house.

"The light," said Cord.

Jimmy Steve found the switch, flicked it.

The ceiling light revealed the bloody mess of the downstairs, intersecting lines of blood like chemtrails tracing the sky, in and out of connecting rooms and leading up the stairs.

Jimmy Steve went to the truck and came back carrying the bent little red toolbox.

They went to work, connecting wires and cameras, drilling, screwing, patching.

While they worked Cord again talked about his plan to invent Alien Fencing and add it to their repertoire of security services.

"It'd be like sky fence," he said. "Shit like that, you know? But 'vis'ble."

"You mean in-visible, dipshit."

"That's what I said, 'visible."

"Yep," said Jimmy Steve, leaning into his drill and firing it up.

"There's aliens," said Jimmy Steve after the whrrr died.

"Yep," said Cord.

"And nobody's gonna want 'em here," said Jimmy Steve.

"Nope."

They both paused their work to look at the radio on the floor as the station went from country music to the local news and the announcer told about how someone had died.

"Possibly horribly murdered," the announcer said as Jimmy Steve and Cord North turned back to their work.

"Hmm, mmm," said the co-announcer just as Jimmy Steve started up a machine that sounded powerful when you used it inside.

Chapter THREE

Think of every big or small innovation that we use today, it came out from the mind of a person who said "there must be a way to do this."

Cord North sat in the pickup, which served as his office for his security systems business as well as his marijuana dealership, as well as his home.

It was cold out, kind of cold, getting cold, toward that time of year when it's cold.

He sat in the library lot, the only vehicle, it must have been closed today.

The radio played.

Cord worked his phone, playing Solitaire with one hand while smoking with the other.

On his lap sat a list of things he had to order for the white house job.

He looked up out the crack of the window and out at the bushes of the property across the alley.

What does it say about me, he thought, that I feel more comfortable around my little cousins, all girls, than around the guys at the bar? At least they are smart, funny, rebellious, contrary, edgy. The guys, well, shit.

The radio announcer talked about people dying, but not anywhere near the library parking lot, yet.

People were missing and Cord pictured for a moment the photos of the colored kids on the wall when you come into Walmart.

Cord reshuffled the computer game and imagined himself a secret agent, for unknown countries and planets, unborn people, doing his best here in these times with what he had to work with.

Cord had the full compliment of worries as anyone, but had been trying to live in the now like someone on TV said might help.

Genius is only appreciated after you are gone, like with his alien fencing, but he could use the money if it could possibly work pretty soon.

He pushed the butt out the little crack and rolled the window down when it landed on the window ledge.

He heard a single winter sparrow tweeting as he rolled the window back up tight.

Cord found a pencil stub and scribbled some figures on the rusty yellow note pad.

He smiled when it came out and then rubbed and crossed out.

"That's not right."

A black and white police car slowly pulled into the parking lot, rolling back and forth at the edge of the drive, inching around the empty lot, shining the outside light all around in the bright sunlight.

It crawled in front of then around Cord North in his pickup, blowing smoke, figuring, erasing, tuning the radio.

Cord noticed single cars here and there pulling into the lot and parking. A woman with waist-length grey hair and a long skirt toted a big flower-pattern cloth purse and a heavy chain of keys toward the front door.

People started to gather there.

A fighter jet whooshed over at tree-top level, as a National Guard Humvee, troop carrier, heavy equipment flatbed, jeep, a children's ice cream buggy, all in desert camo, rolled past.

Cord decided to go inside the library to get warm, save on gas, and wait for Jimmy Steve to show.

He paused at the bulletin board looking for home security competition.

He spotted one business card, snatched it, crunched it inside his fist and dropped it to the floor with a muffled insurgent clatter.

Cord moved through the automatic glass doors and the security machine.

He passed the Time Magazine and Newsweek Magazine displays with the historical covers of the smiling, handsome dead brothers, the moon, the reverend.

Live in the moment.

The thought kept running through Cord's mind for some reason and it made him think of bad things in the past and bad things in the future, to come.

Cord found the newest edition of Modern Security and sat on a hard chair to read.

He saw a kid walking by on the sidewalk and thought, that kid walking home on the side of the road, by heavy traffic, in that boy lies the world, it's not ruined, not yet, it's still there, the wonder and the possibility still live.

And he felt something in his back.

Poking.

He turned around, scowling.

He didn't like to be poked in the back, right there, high up.

Jimmy Steve stood with the piece they had been waiting for, the last part of the puzzle, so to speak, as to how they were going to secure this home, their new invention that would take them to the top of the home security rat race.

Jimmy Steve's cousin had finally come home from the west coast run and unlocked his garage and showed it to Jimmy Steve.

He also had a parking ticket that he had found on Cord's windshield. He handed it over as well.

"Cool," said Cord.

Chapter FOUR

"A meeting is that measure whereby a large number of people gather and some say things that they don't think and others think things that they don't say."
— Vladimir Voinovich, The Life and Extraordinary Adventures of Private Ivan Chonkin

These are the people you see walking through the neighborhood in the morning, in single file, awkwardly, hands out for balance, smiling, muttering to the one ahead to keep going.

They have walked this sidewalk since it was new, now they know each bump and chip and danger, older people carrying Superman lunch boxes. RE-tards. Re-TARDS. The emphasis, depending.

These are the people who work at the group homes and the workshops, day programs, women most, who drop their own children off at daycare at seven and nurse smoking Oldsmobiles while lighting a last cigarette of the early morning on the way.

These are the people who don't have to give a shit. Who it's hard to say much about because who are they, where are they? They have mansions ringing the lake, slide in and out of reality in sleek machines.

These are the people whose mothers drank to survive while they struggled as well, and the fathers, pollution in the water, something else, but what? Why are they like they are? The curse of the almighty? The love of God? They go to church and to the park in white vans and they sit in clumps at a movie.

These are the people who trod the tile of Walmart, all day long, pushing the cart that carries the child that wants the dog that needs the food that costs the money that is hard to get in order to bump and waddle amid the wares of Walmart.

These are the people, named Stuart and Sue and Bo and Jean who stutter a little, who smile and touch, who learn to cook at fifty, to fold their clothes, to make their bed, to go out for pizza while holding hands, then brush your front teeth forty times and off to bed.

"One, two, three, four ... "

These are the people who step outside the bar to smoke, in a hurry, talking fast, day not done, what a week it's been.

These are all the people. Who work in the restaurants, hotels and convenience stores.

These are the people with thousands, millions, billions, homes, cars, big dogs, boats, what else?

Everything.

Who own the people smoking in the glow of the neon lights, hold their pounding hearts in the palm of their hands and can choose to either squeeze or let them live today, to stutter and bump and waddle within the walls of Walmart.

Chapter FIVE

*"Like so many Americans, she was trying to construct a
life that made sense from things she found in gift shops."*
— *Kurt Vonnegut,* Slaughterhouse-Five

"Welcome to Earth Burger, would you like a pistachio malt, or a lemon cake or large home fries? Do you have a member's card? Earth to No. 312. How may I help you?"

Chrystena adjusted her headpiece and addressed the next customer.

Tena was in the ninth hour of a six-hour shift on the drive-through window.

"Did I say I want fries. Did I say I want to super-size? When I say it, you will be the first to know it."

"I have to be at work in six minutes. Six minutes! Do you know how long is six minutes!"

"Yes ma'am."

"Six fucking minutes! Can you even hear me? Where are you? Where the hell is my food!"

"This is not my order. Do I look like I would order this much food? Who can eat this much food? No, no, I'll just take it. Do you take checks?"

"Those are beautiful ear rings."

"Thank you."

"You're so pretty."

"Thank you."

"Can you see me? I can see you. I'm psychic. I see and know all."

"That must be time consuming."

"What time is it? Do you have the time in there?"

"One-thirty-two."

"Oh, thank you. My little girl has a doctor's appointment. We've been waiting so long to get in, they don't like welfare patients somebody said, anyway, we don't have ... we'll come back."

"I'll bring your order out. Pull ahead of the line and park by the yellow sign."

"Oh, thank you so much."

"How do you get to Walmart?"

"Can I get a cigarette?"

"I don't smoke, sorry."

"Is it s'posed to rain?"

"I'm out of gas.

"I am out of gas.

"I am out of gas.

"Are you fucking kidding me? I am out of gas?"

"I don't have no money. My purse is at home. Really. I'm sorry. Here. Take it back."

"No. That's okay. Here. We're good. No worries!"

"I am late for work. Can you hurry!

"Ha-llo-o! Anybody in there!"

CHAPTER SIX

"America is the wealthiest nation on Earth, but its people are mainly poor, and poor Americans are urged to hate themselves. It is in fact a crime for an American to be poor, even though America is a nation of poor."
— *Kurt Vonnegut,* Slaughterhouse-Five

Cord North sat with his father at the nursing home, outside at the table in the sun and the chilled air, wearing light jackets and orange hunting hats.

Cord mostly listened, nodding, fidgeting, looking here and there.

We were students, fucking stupid kids once.

With the Vietnam war was coming down on our heads – our deaths – why didn't we care? We also thought we would not live long because of Cold War – nuclear war imminent, but not too important.

Apparently.

Not in my town. Maybe in other towns, not mine, not that I remember.

Was it because of Saturday Night Live, Monday Night Football, Sunday's 60 Minutes?

Little House on the Prairie, Gunsmoke? The Andy Griffith Show, The Brady Bunch? Hee-Haw, Happy Days, The Beverly Hillbillies, I Dream of Jeannie, Dallas?

The Waltons, Three's Company, Wheel of Fortune?

Hawaii Five-O, All In The Family, Mission Impossible, The Dukes of Hazzard?

I know the theme music and the characters of all a them, but I don't

remember why we weren't afraid of dying on TV, on The Six O'Clock News.
    We drank, drove around, drank some more, played games.
    We were going to die.
    It was all on TV.
    We didn't seem to care.
    What the hell?
    I haven't thought of it 'til now.
    I wonder why.

Chapter SEVEN

"Morale was deteriorating and it was all Yossarian's fault. The country was in peril; he was jeopardizing his traditional rights of freedom and independence by daring to exercise them."

— Joseph Heller, Catch-22

If you see something, say something.

The town sign on both sides of Middle Street implored.

If everyone watched out, they would all live forever, all be happy forever, if everyone did their part.

Two men had stayed after the burial ceremony and sat on gravestones, talking.

They talked about heart pills and stomach pills and head pills, doctor appointments, safe drinking and driving and home repair and car maintenance and how their grandkids just like to mess with that temperature gauge when they aren't looking.

"Up to 73!"

"Yeah, I know."

The houses were mostly the same shape, colors, pastel, bungalows, small, steeply pitched roofs, close together, big front and back yards.

An obvious company town to a tourist, maybe not so much to someone here sixty years.

Built to bring in human beings to live their lives and make money for the company.

Still, lives none-the-less.
Signs scattered here and there.
"We Support Mining."

Chapter EIGHT

"Why aren't you in school? I see you every day wandering around."

"Oh, they don't miss me," she said. "I'm antisocial, they say. I don't mix. It's so strange. I'm very social indeed. It all depends on what you mean by social, doesn't it? Social to me means talking to you about things like this."

"... Or talking about how strange the world is. Being with people is nice. But I don't think it's social to get a bunch of people together and then not let them talk, do you? An hour of TV class, an hour of basketball or baseball or running, another hour of transcription history or painting pictures, and more sports, but do you know, we never ask questions, or at least most don't; they just run the answers at you, bing, bing, bing, and us sitting there for four more hours of film-teacher. That's not social to me at all. It's a lot of funnels and lot of water poured down the spout and out the bottom, and them telling us it's wine when it's not. They run us so ragged by the end of the day we can't do anything but go to bed or head for a Fun Park to bully people around, break windowpanes in the Window Smasher place or wreck cars in the Car Wrecker place with the big steel ball. Or go out in the cars and race on the streets, trying to see how close you can get to lampposts, playing 'chicken' and 'knock hubcaps.' I guess I'm everything they say I am, all right. I haven't any friends. That's supposed to prove I'm abnormal. But everyone I know is either shouting or dancing around like

94

wild or beating up one another. Do you notice how people hurt each other nowadays?"

— Ray Bradbury, Fahrenheit 451

A very young couple walked down a rez road.
One native, the girl white, with child.

They laughed, touched hands, held hands, laughed more, walk along the side of the road, headed to the store for milk and bread. They walked a mile, two miles. They waved to their friends in the yards, kept walking, his hand now around her waist.

Nobody knew of them except their many friends and relatives. There are millions and millions and millions of people who do not care about them, who would not care even if they knew about them, except if they came to know them, then they would love them.

They were smart, aware, told cutting edge jokes to each other in knowing whispers.

And at the end of this road nobody knew them.

Nobody cared.

They would never be on The Price Is Right or The Tonight Show or sing the song before the ballgame or get re-tweeted or have a hundred hits on their blog.

The Nightly News would only mention them if they were said to have done something really, really wrong.

All they had was this, what they could see in front of them.

Their whole life was in front of them.

And they seemed to be happy.

Their names were Joe Black Bear and Mary Ann Thomas.

CHAPTER NINE

"Insanity is contagious."

— *Joseph Heller,* Catch-22

Randy, Philip, Todd, Jesse: The Banks Brothers.

Wynnie, Wendy, Wanda, Winona, Whitney, Wilma, Whitley: The Storm Sisters.

The town website said Home Security Capital of The World, because of the Banks boys and Storm girls, "who took the high school class of Mr. Bobb's woodshop and went on to become the Washington D.C. Security Savantz, and the Security Of The Starz, in Hollywood, California."

The Banks boys owned the home Cord and Jimmy Steve were working on. They want Cord to tell everyone and the word will spread across the nation – and they will be able to crack down with more police and they also want to, in the course of things, accomplish their main objective, without it being noticed very much — defeat their rivals from across the alley – the fucking Storm sisters, wipe their names for all time off the town website, along with promoting their own business, their specialties being turmoil, tumult, trouble and terror.

And of course, the Storms were not just lying around waiting to be attacked.

They were also busy, drumming up business through their specialties, fomenting "apprehension, confusion, and disruption of daily routine."

CHAPTER TEN

*"They agreed that it was neither possible nor necessary
to educate people who never questioned anything."*
— *Joseph Heller,* Catch-22

It had been discovered or rumored or remotely viewed that there were bodies in the forest.

And that there were bodies in the park.

As well as bodies floating on the water.

Some said that those were just shadows, images, reflections that came from the shirts and jackets and pants and sweatshirts on Mrs. Kapourek's clothesline.

Even atop the water, shadows, glimmering.

Those people had gone away.

Chapter ELEVEN

"What a lousy earth! He wondered how many people were destitute that same night even in his own prosperous country, how many homes were shanties, how many husbands were drunk and wives socked, and how many children were bullied, abused, or abandoned. How many families hungered for food they could not afford to buy? How many hearts were broken? How many suicides would take place that same night, how many people would go insane? How many cockroaches and landlords would triumph? How many winners were losers, successes failures, and rich men poor men? How many wise guys were stupid? How many happy endings were unhappy endings? How many honest men were liars, brave men cowards, loyal men traitors, how many sainted men were corrupt, how many people in positions of trust had sold their souls to bodyguards, how many had never had souls? How many straight-and-narrow paths were crooked paths? How many best families were worst families and how many good people were bad people? When you added them all up and then subtracted, you might be left with only the children, and perhaps with Albert Einstein and an old violinist or sculptor somewhere."

— Joseph Heller, Catch 22

Cord North lay on the hood of his pickup, looking up at the stars. I care when some die, do not give ... a ... fuck when others die. I wonder why that is.

I care when bears die, when they put pictures in the newspaper of bears killed by hunters, and that makes me mad.

When they talk about cops killed or soldiers or guards, I could give a shit. Not at all, except that little bit that tingles.

I want to rock-solid know something nobody else does. Something big. I could live just on that. I wouldn't tell anybody, just walk around knowing it.

Once I tried to get a job on a Chinese ship, a big ship, a monster, but they said they only took Chinese. I wonder who I would be now if I got that job. Would I be me?

I seen a Bigfoot. I thought it was someone and I waved. It didn't wave back so I walked up to it to ask why it would not wave. My mind is wiped clear but I think what happened is I thought it was a bear and I ran. Then I looked back and it walked like a man and I went back and put out my hand to shake and said, my name's Cord, then it stepped back, put up its hands, crouched low, growled deep, showed me its teeth and red eyes and I thought it was the devil.

I ran again. I wonder who I would be now if I had not ran.

Once I seen a UFO, an orange light, not too far away. I was driving, it was a little bit ahead of me and it kept the distance, I kept going, staring, not sure what I was thinking, probably freaking, then it shot straight out, not up, but along the ground, parallel to it, became smaller real fast. I don't know what it was, but wouldn't you say that was a UFO? I wonder who I would be now if they had stopped and talked to me.

In high school somebody, a counselor I guess, asked me what I wanted to do, to be? I didn't know, so I said, businessman. I had no fucking idea. So focused on my face and being paranoid and my weight and being scared that I hadn't thought about it. I didn't have time.

The Beatles interviews are the most amazing thing I ever seen. Their sincerity, humility, humor, and so much more, in the face of all of this. All this, is like the people around them. It's a goddamned species difference between the four Beatles and the reporters around them. No wonder we liked them. They were us. They weren't different. They were just like us, what we wanted to be, what we saw ourselves as being. Just like JFK.

I'm just done with it. I've tried it and practiced and practiced and that's enough. I can't do it anymore, all these things I'm doing just because I think I should, music, learning another language, tying my shoes, eating bread and drinking my milk. We do not need milk. No fucking more.

I thought I wanted to do so much when I was older when I was ten, now that I'm here I don't know what I'll do.

He felt something in his back and reached around.

He found a piece of ripped up paper under the driver's side wiper.

It was a coupon for half-priced kiwi-strawberry malts at Earth Burger.

"Niiice," Cord hummed as he leaned back again.

Chapter TWELVE

"When Švejk subsequently described life in the lunatic asylum, he did so in exceptionally eulogistic terms: 'I really don't know why those loonies get so angry when they're kept there. You can crawl naked on the floor, howl like a jackal, rage and bite. If anyone did this anywhere on the promenade people would be astonished, but there it's the most common or garden thing to do. There's a freedom there which not even Socialists have ever dreamed of."
— *Jaroslav Hašek,* The Good Soldier Švejk

They sat.

Somehow they had gotten there and since they were they sat.

The chairs displayed a variety of opinions of what it meant to be close enough to the table.

The hands touched the white mugs.

Cars outside at pumps, people buying coffee and muffins in clear bags.

A repeating Broadway play, same lines, scenery, players.

Has run for years, day after day after day after day.

"Hey."

"How goes it?"

"How's the car?"

"I'm a Ford man."

"No! I've never heard that."

The script does not vary, no matter what is happening around it, in the muffin line, at the pumps, on the highway, on the horizon.

There are three trails leading to the store. You can touch one, with a foot, a toe, a heal, a metal pole. We ask you in the names of your grandchildren, don't ever touch the third.

There are three quails sitting outside on the curb. Touch two if you want, not that third one.

There are three tails, three behinds of three old ladies in the muffin line. Touch two if you want, but never touch the third.

There are three ales sitting close by. Touch two, go ahead, go on. Do not touch the third.

There are three nails right there, within reach.

There are three sails, outside, on three boats. Yes, you may get up, go outside, slip on your coat, we will wait for you. Yes, it's windy, but you said you wanted to go.

But remember.

There are three pails, whales, veils and snails, inside the store, outside and around the table.

Touch two if you must, but never ... ever touch the third.

The players never touch the third quail, the third whale, veil or snail, never-ever-ever.

They understand that the survival of the play depends upon it and they love the play.

They love the play.

All around them disease and war and it does not ever invade the stage.

The stage is the stage.

The players the players.

And they love the play.

Chapter THIRTEEN

"... But then he listed the countries and regions of the world where people were wallowing in poverty and ignorance, some not even knowing what electricity and toilet paper were, and yet they had among them an immense number of bards, minstrels and other varieties of fold or court poets. The authorities there regard the state of the poetic word with anxious concern and good poets (who write good words about the authorities) are generally rewarded with all sorts of good things, whereas bad poets (who write bad words about the authorities) have their heads cut off. The risk of being left without a head can act as such a powerful stimulus to the mind that on occasion bad poets write much better poetry than good poets and people copy the poems of bad poets into notebooks, learn them by heart and transmit them from one generation to the next."

— Monumental Propaganda, Vladimir Voinovich

"Welcome to The Feud!"

Name something you would say to someone who tries to tell you about a "conspiracy theory."

"Survey says!"

Stay on the same page!

Good answer!

Bring it to the table.

Good answer!
Oh, brother!
Good answer!
At the end of the day!
Good answer!
I get all that, but ...
Good answer!

Chapter FOURTEEN

"'At Sarajevo in Bosnia, Mr. Palivec. They've just shot His Imperial Highness, the Archduke Ferdinand, there. What do you say to that?

"'I don't poke my nose into things like that. They can kiss my arse if I do!'" Palivec replied politely, lighting his pipe. "'Nowadays, if anyone got mixed up in a business like that, he'd risk breaking his neck. I'm a tradesman and when anyone comes in here and orders a beer I fill up his glass. But Sarajevo, politics or the late lamented Archduke are nothing for people like us. They lead straight to Pankrac.'"

— Jaroslav Hašek, The Good Soldier Švejk

They sit in their chairs, sneaking looks.
The food fills the tray, called a TV tray, most appropriately.
The National Six O'clock News.
People have died. People are dying. People are gonna die.
"More food."
"Mmmmm."
"It's good."

CHAPTER FIFTEEN

"The best thing you can do ... is to pretend to be an idiot."
— *Jaroslav Hašek,* The Good Soldier Švejk

How about the team?
They talk.
Something to talk about.
Inside the stadium.
At work.
The water cooler.
Something safe.
Keep us safe.
Urinals.

A bakery truck, many trucks, with happy, colorful lettering, both sides — "Call Us! We're Already There!" — round the corner, many, many corners, two tires, screeching.

Somewhere an elephant trumpets as the players take the field.

Chapter SIXTEEN

"Americans, like human beings everywhere, believe many things that are obviously untrue. Their most destructive untruth is that it is very easy for any American to make money. They will not acknowledge how in fact hard money is to come by, and, therefore, those who have no money blame and blame and blame themselves. This inward blame has been a treasure for the rich and powerful, who have had to do less for their poor, publicly and privately, than any other ruling class since, say Napoleonic times. Many novelties have come from America. The most startling of these, a thing without precedent, is a mass of undignified poor. They do not love one another because they do not love themselves."

— *Kurt Vonnegut,* Slaughterhouse-Five

Cord North sat on the hood of his truck, chillaxing, leaning back on the windshield, looking up at the stars, now releasing the smoke.

I will lose, but I won't quit.

My personality fucking dissolves, evaporates, when many loud people take over a room.

Is there real generosity? Or do you give something always just to get something back?

If someone wanted to and knew how, with just saying things, I know I could be driven stark raving crazy in twenty minutes.

There's people who have seen things when they're alone – strange things, but don't talk about them and when they do talk about them, well what can be done with stories like that, even if someone did kind of believe them? I know, right? Well, I saw a missile in S.D. I was just walking along a gravel road and here it came over a field about tree height, straight, parallel, and when it came to me it shut straight up, did a loop de loop, continued perfectly along its path. I wonder were they practicing for something? And I picked up a hitchhiker once. He said he had been taken from an orphanage by government people and some things done to him. He was in Vietnam, specially trained to kill and when a certain commercial came on the TV he was trained to react. It was like a Clairol commercial or some shit. And are these things keys to understanding our world, along with the UFO and the Bigfoot? How do I know. I'll never forget, but what can I do with stories like that, but drag them around with me, in and out of Walmart, Dairy Queen, Kwik Trip, ya know. Shit.

Animals in a cage and we are miserable – someone else gets our food, we don't make our own homes, do nothing for ourselves.

CHAPTER SEVENTEEN

"We believe the lies because to not do so would result in cognitive dissonance. To avoid the insanity of cognitive dissonance, we have gone insane with fear — of terrorism, for sure, but the old bugaboos are still around: drugs, homosexuals, pagans ...

"After all, "a normal person understands that it's dangerous and pointless to oppose universal insanity, and rational to participate in it. It should also be noted that people are all actors, and many of them easily adapt to the role written for them out of fear or in hopes of a worthwhile reward."

— http://www.curledup.com/monuprop.htm

Plane crash.
In the forest.
Terrible.
Do you understand what happens to a human body when ...?
Blood. Skin. Fluids.
I mean in just a car crash at sixty it's unimaginable if you haven't, you know, well.
Rain. Freezing rain, clouds.
Some say?
He died.
Who?
Him.
No!
Not him!

Him, exactly him. His photo is on the internet.

All?

And there is this kid who walks around his block on the side of the road, by heavy traffic.

In that boy lies the world, it's not ruined, not yet, it's still there, the wonder and the possibility still live.

Not.

It's just a dumbass walking with one foot in the grass and one on the blacktop, going in a circle he thinks is the world.

"You are so mean."

I am just saying the truth.

There are at least two ways of looking at things.

They are not equal.

Even though there are two, one is right, one is wrong.

You are stupid if you do not see that.

Then I guess I am just stupid.

Yes.

You are.

CHAPTER EIGHTEEN

"It was miraculous. It was almost no trick at all, he saw, to turn vice into virtue and slander into truth, impotence into abstinence, arrogance into humility, plunder into philanthropy, thievery into honor, blasphemy into wisdom, brutality into patriotism, and sadism into justice. Anybody could do it; it required no brains at all. It merely required no character."

— *Joseph Heller,* Catch-22

Lies. Like flies.
In the air.
We suck them in, chew it, piss and shit it out.
Subsistence, enough to live?
Maybe today. Yes, true, yesterday, but not tomorrow.
For years and years.
We subsist.
But it's not really living.

Chapter NINETEEN

"You tell me that he's a fool, but he's got such a huge head, it must be full of something."

"Yes, it's full of foolishness," the Admiral said ruthlessly. Let me tell you something. You've probably been out in the country. You may have noticed that every village has one idiot and one wise man. Some simple peasant. With a head the size of your fist and a brain that's probably not very big. But he thinks simply, clearly and soundly on the basis of his own knowledge of life and personal experience. So what I'd advise you to learn is this. The human brain is distinguished not only by its dimensions, but by its ability to assimilate input. The brain, crudely speaking, can be a warehouse, a mill or a chemical laboratory. A warehouse can be really vast and stocked with various kinds of items, but the more items there are, the harder it is to make sense of them. A mill can only grind up whatever is poured into it. It may be small and primitive, but it will still grind good grain into pretty good flour. But even if you take a big, modern mill, the very finest, with good grindstones and ideal sieves and load it up with bad grain, it won't turn out anything, that's any good. The creative brain is the highest type, a chemical laboratory – load anything you like into it and it produces something fundamentally new, a synthesis. Everything in it works: knowledge, memory, the capacity for independent thought. That kind of brain is very rare,

even among people with big heads."
  — *Vladimir Voinovich,* Monumental Propaganda

Cord and Jimmy Steve parked in the big, empty lot, walked into the mall.

One and then the other paused at the window of the electronics store, before they would go in.

They couldn't hear what was being said on the color TVs in the big clean window.

They recognized the leader on one set and the Disney characters on the other two.

They had been staring at the sun sitting on the hood of the pickup and they stared back and forth, watching a tennis match and the characters and the leader become blurred.

They each held in their hands copies of the same candidate flyer that had been under both wipers on the pickup. They had forgotten they had them until now. They let go the flyers like poop.

Remembering what they had talked about or maybe getting rid of it.

The real world is not dog eat dog, but symbiotic, cooperative.

They moved their eyes and heads just a little, enough to create a blur, and it was fun at first.

For a while they liked it and then they didn't and they decided without announcing it that it was time to go inside the store.

With their new invention from the one cousin, to see if the electronics store might be interested.

On the way they had talked about all the things they would do when their invention made them rich.

"We'll be set, just sit back, set for life, sit around, all day. And do nothing. Yeah. What? Yeah, I guess that'd be okay."

The high school kid in the store says he doesn't know.

"It's just glow sticks.

"That's already been invented, 'cause, like, here it is."

"I know, right?" said Jimmy Steve and Cord gave him a look.

They leave, pass the TVs without looking, sit down on a bench in the middle of the mall, watching the people who come to the wishing well and toss in money.

They read the T-shirts on the people.

"I've never been on a hayride"

"There's nothing in the world like an Oreo cookie with some cold milk"

"I get that. I get all that."
"Got Cognitive Dissonance?"
"Got serotonin?
"I don't know why but I just thought of Lawrence Welk"
"Does anyone still play Chinese Checkers?"
"If you've seen one fireworks show you've seen them all"
"I can't remember the last time I went to a zoo"
"I like Donald Duck better than Mickey Mouse."

Chapter TWENTY

"Still and all, why bother? Here's my answer. Many people need desperately to receive this message: I feel and think much as you do, care about many of the things you care about, although most people do not care about them. You are not alone."

— *Kurt Vonnegut*

"Welcome to Earth Burger, would you like a lemon malt, or a pistachio cake or large curly fries? Do you have a member's card? Earth to No. 92. How may I help you?"

Chrystena adjusted her headpiece and addressed the next customer.

Tena was in the sixth hour of a six-hour shift on the drive-through window.

Cord and Jimmy Steve pulled through, too far, backed up.

Hey.

Hey.

Hey.

Tena is Jimmy Steve's cousin.

Just minutes before, Jimmy Steve ran. Ran up to Cord to tell him they had striked it rich!

They talked about needing to expand the business because they had gotten another customer.

"Well," said Cord.

He talked about the different options they had, zero and none.

"I don't know what to say, really," he said.

"You could move into my garage," Tena said.
"Okay."
"Cool."

CHAPTER TWENTY-ONE

"That's the good part of dying; when you've nothing to lose, you run any risk you want."
— Ray Bradbury, Fahrenheit 451

Yes, Cord and Jimmy Steve striked it rich.

So they drove the pickup head-first into Tena's driveway up to her garage.

They carried inside the glow sticks, a grungy yellow legal pad they found under the seat, the pen, the red tool box and a carton of cigarettes.

"That's it?" said Tena.

"Yes."

"Mmm, hmm."

And yes, the fucking glow sticks invention was just glow sticks, but they thought of something on their own on the hood of the pickup looking up at the stars.

They had all the cousins thinking of a good name for it.

Super insoles to sneak up on a burglar, fire extinguisher, white coverall disaster suit and plastic goggles – nobody they knew of sold them all as a set – you would have to go to lots of different places and you'd have to think of that and who would do that.

With a glow stick that they were calling a mini-light saber for the junior security agent of the household.

And the next day they took out a loan from the cousins and drove all around to the different stores, back to the garage and organized all the stuff into sets and arranged them by the side door of the garage, off the cement on a pallet they found on the dump road.

"Cool," said Tena.

"You guys are all set, seeya."

"You know what we'd really fuckin' like?" said Cord.

So, Tena knew somebody, someone she had done a favor for in the drive-through line.

And that person worked in the city offices see.

And she put Cord and Jimmy Steve on the website wearing full security gear, the white suits and hoodies and holding all the new gear, fire extinguishers, glow sticks, "silent sneakers," plastic goggles and snorkles and she erased the Banks Brothers and Storm Sisters and now the website said:

"HOME OF 'Your Home Our Home Security Systmz'"

CHAPTER TWENTY-TWO

"If you don't want a man unhappy politically, don't give him two sides to a question to worry him; give him one. Better yet, give him none. Let him forget there is such a thing as war. If the government is inefficient, top-heavy, and tax-mad, better it be all those than that people worry over it. Peace, Montag. Give the people contests they win by remembering the words to more popular songs or the names of state capitals or how much corn Iowa grew last year. Cram them full of noncombustible data, chock them so damned full of 'facts' they feel stuffed, but absolutely 'brilliant' with information. Then they'll feel they're thinking, they'll get a sense of motion without moving. And they'll be happy, because facts of that sort don't change."

— *Ray Bradbury,* Fahrenheit 451

Cord sat in the office on the metal chair.

He looked up as the light came in when the door opened and Jimmy Steve marched across the concrete carrying a little piece of paper that he held out toward Cord.

Cord reached up and took it even though he saw that Jimmy Steve was crying.

He read it and bowed his head.

Northern Pooper was dead, hit head-on by a Bell GoPro Phantom 2 Quadcopter Drone. The whole thing was captured on the drone video and had ninety-two thousand views on Youtube.

Jimmy Steve held out his other hand, the one with "fuck" on it in old ink.

Another note? said Cord's wet eyes.

He grabbed it like an executive with too much going on.

"Psst," said the note from the white house home owners.

"It was paint and like Halloween makeup, the house, to clean up, you know, right?"

"I get all that," said Cord looking up at Jimmy Steve standing way too close right above him.

Tena stepped over the side door threshold and walked in the sunlight path like a morning angel in her Earth Burger uniform toward Cord and Jimmy Steve.

She smiled and headed right for the wall and plopped down on the hard, red and white bench back seat her cousins had brought in from an old Ford in the backyard weeds.

"Hey," she said as she tried to bounce.

"Whatdya think, hey?"

"Hey," said Cord.

"Can I stay here?"

"Yeah," she said.

"Yeah, sure."

A REPORTER'S LIFE

by Mike Palecek

All great ideas are controversial, or have been at one time.

I am merely trying to illustrate one of the fundamental facts about American journalism today, the fact that the servants of the press lords are slaves very much as they have always been, and that any attempt at revolt is immediately punished with the economic weapon.

But much more vicious than these cases is the majority of foreign correspondents who never have to be placed against the wall, who are never told what to write and how to write it, but who know from contact with the great minds of the press lords or from the simple deduction that the bosses are in big business and the news must be slanted accordingly, or from the general intangible atmosphere which prevails everywhere, what they can do and what they must never do. The most stupid boast in the history of present-day journalism is that of the writer who says, "I have never been given orders; I am free to do as I like."

— George Seldes

Journalists are revolutionaries. You have to fight to change the world.
— Gary Webb

You have to fight a little bit for democracy every day.

The assassination mystery is so important that every American citizen should become involved.
— Penn Jones, Jr.

JUNE 22, 1967

I am not the first editor to comment on the similarity of the United States to that of Germany of 1936 or 1937. What our citizens do during the next few years will determine just how far along the pattern of Germany we go. And the citizens must make the wise and all important decisions with almost no guidance of the editors or clergy.

In fact, the editors seem determined to do all they can to rush the country along Hitler's vicious path.

The clergy, as usual, remains slavishly silent.

To review where we find ourselves today, we will recount some of the glaring efforts being made to thwart the work being done to discover who killed the President of the United States in 1963.

... PUBLISHED MAY 25, 1967

Immediately after the assassination in Dallas, the public was helping with a constant stream of information — much more than the authorities had anticipated. People were volunteering clues at an alarming rate, and it had to stop. The Dallas police told one man to: "Go home and forget it." The FBI told one man: "If you didn't see Oswald shoot out that sixth floor window, you had better keep your damn mouth sh..!t."

(Midlothian Mirror, Midlothian, Texas)
— Penn Jones, Jr.

If most writers are honest with themselves, this is the difference they want to make: before, they were not noticed; now they are.
— Tom Wolfe

If you gather a lot of stuff, then you write it, write in scenes with dialogue. Somewhere in the middle, rising from all this research like strong metal towers, is your opinions.

... When you stop drinking, you have to deal with this marvelous personality that started you drinking in the first place.

... Rage is the only quality which has kept me, or anybody I have ever studied, writing columns for newspapers.

— Jimmy Breslin

Look, I went into journalism to do journalism, not advertising.

— Michael Hastings

... Yet who is he who could stand a hundred unanswered questions and answer none? An unanswered question flutters about you for the rest of your life. It does not let you sleep; it does not let you think. You feel that the equilibrium of the universe is at stake if you leave a question pending. A question without an answer is something so incomplete that you simply cannot bear it. You can get crazy thinking of the problems of an unbalanced solar system. The word 'Why' with a question mark behind it is the cause, I am quite certain, of all culture, civilization, progress, and science. This word 'Why' has changed and will again change every system by which mankind lives and prospers; it will end war, and it will bring war again; it will lead to communism, and it will surely destroy communism again; it will make dictators and despots, and it will dethrone them again; it will make new religions, and it will turn them into superstitions again; it will make a nebula the real and the spiritual center of the universes, and it will again make the same nebula an insignificant speck in the super-universe. The little word 'Why'? with a question mark.

— B. Traven, "The Death Ship"

I'm onto a big story, and need to go off the [radar] for a bit.
All the best, and hope to see you all soon.

— Michael Hastings email fifteen hours before dying in a fiery car crash at 4:30 a.m. in Los Angeles

... The writer must be a participant in the scene ... like a film director who writes his own scripts, does his own camera work, and somehow manages to film himself in action, as the protagonist or at least the main character.

... There is no such thing as paranoia. Your worst fears can come true at any moment.

... As things stand now, I am going to be a writer. I'm not sure that I'm going to be a good one or even a self-supporting one, but until the dark thumb of fate presses me to the dust and says 'you are nothing', I will be a writer."

... I find that by putting things in writing I can understand them and see them a little more objectively ... For words are merely tools and if you use the right ones you can actually put even your life in order, if you don't lie to yourself and use the wrong words.

... Events of the past two years have virtually decreed that I shall wrestle with the literary muse for the rest of my days. And so, having tasted the poverty of one end of the scale, I have no choice but to direct my energies toward the acquisition of fame and fortune. Frankly, I have no taste for either poverty or honest labor, so writing is the only recourse left me.

— Hunter S. Thompson

I never type in the morning. I don't get up in the morning. I drink at night. I try to stay in bed until twelve o'clock, that's noon. Usually, if I have to get up earlier, I don't feel good all day. I look, if it says twelve, then I get up and my day begins. I eat something, and then I usually run right up to the race track after I wake up. I bet the horses, then I come back and Linda cooks something and we talk awhile, we eat, and we have a few drinks, and then I go upstairs with a couple of bottles and I type — starting around nine-thirty and going until one-thirty, two-thirty at night.
And that's it.

... unless it comes out of your soul like a rocket, unless being still would drive you to madness or suicide or murder, don't do it.
... unless the sun inside you is burning in your gut, don't do it.
... when it is truly time, and if you have been chosen, it will do it by

itself and it will
   keep on doing it until you die or it dies in you.
                                        — Charles Bukowski

   No one in this world, so far as I know ... has ever lost money by
underestimating the intelligence of the great masses of the plain
people. Nor has anyone ever lost public office thereby. The mistake that
is made always runs the other way. Because the plain people are able
to speak and understand, and even, in many cases, to read and write,
it is assumed that they have ideas in their heads, and an appetite for
more. The assumption is a folly. They dislike ideas, for ideas make them
uncomfortable.
                                        — H.L. Mencken

   The only kinds of fights worth fighting are those you are going to lose,
because somebody has to fight them and lose and lose and lose until
someday, somebody who believes as you do wins. In order for somebody
to win an important, major fight 100 years hence, a lot of other people
have got to be willing — for the sheer fun and joy of it — to go right ahead
and fight, knowing you're going to lose. You mustn't feel like a martyr.
You've got to enjoy it.
                                        — I.F. Stone

   There is a willful desire on the part of those in positions of authority
to keep the masses down, to involve us in perpetual wars, and to deny
the great majority of Americans true liberty and the pursuit of happiness.
Until the Internet came along, Americans had to rely on the television
networks, daily newspapers, and large circulation magazines for their
information. Now that there are finally true alternative sources available
on the web, the dishonest nature of the mainstream media is brutally
apparent. It's become almost comical to watch these relics from a
bygone era continue to babble on about an absurdly restricted selection
of topics, to control the tenor of debate, and transparently attempt to
manipulate the public, as they were so successful in the past...In the
pages that follow, you'll find an uninterrupted timeline of conspiratorial
activity on the part of our leaders.
                                        — Donald Jeffries

You fail only if you stop writing. You must stay drunk on writing so reality cannot destroy you. You've got to jump off cliffs and build your wings on the way down.

— Ray Bradbury

His goal is not quality journalism.
His goal is vast power for Rupert Murdoch, political power.

— Mike Royko

Are the editorial pages of the New York Times journalism? Yes.
But they're opinion. They're opinion based on fact.
In my case, it's going to take somebody 20 or 30 years to
figure out what I came up with, because while it's journalism,
it's also satire coupled with a large sprinkling of opinion to
create a work of art.

— Michael Moore

Jimmy Carter.
Ronald Reagan.
Some choice.
In a country of over 225 million people, are these the two most
intelligent, resourceful, creative, compassionate and visionary persons that can be found to lead this country toward peace, jobs and social justice?
Of course not.
They are inept, incompetent, unimaginative, unstable and beings of lower intelligence.
They are as mediocre as prime time TV — and therein lies their greatest strength.
Creatures of the mass media, they appeal to a country that has come to expect very little from anything, a populace that is satisfied with the bland and the dull.
Dull schools, dull jobs, dull life.
And when election time on November 4 rolls around, over half of the people in this country won't even bother to vote. They will stay at home because they know, regardless of who is elected, their life on November 5 will be the same.

— Michael Moore, The Flint Voice, November 1980

Lenny Bruce is a very moral man trying to improve the world and trying to make audiences think.

— Dorothy Killgallen

O the press, the press, the freedom of the press. They'll never take away the freedom of the press.

We must be free to say whatever's on our chest — with a hey-diddle-dee and ho-nanny-no for whichever side will pay the best.

— "The Cradle Will Rock"

The country is barbarously large and final," ... It is too much country — boondock country –

alternately drab and dazzling, spectral and remote. It is so wrongfully muddled and various that it is difficult to conceive of it all of a piece.

— Billy Lee Brammer, "A Gay Place"

Miss Kilgallen printed information in her column several times about cases involving the FBI, none of which were true.

Dorothy Kilgallen died in November 1965, from alcohol and barbiturates.

— FBI file on Dorothy Killgallen

By Billy Lee Blueberry.

He began.

"He looked up at the sky, as dark as Cookie's coffee dotted everywhere with sugary stars."

That was his novel.

And now he had a first line and the rest shouldn't be so bad.

He could do it.

But did he want to.

Nope.

Billy Lee pushed back on the desk, squeaking his chair over the wood floor.

He had to write.

All around him the walls were just about covered with the framed stories he'd written.

Who Killed JFK.

Who Killed RFK.

Who Killed MLK.

There were stories about the murder of Paul Wellstone, about Oklahoma City, Waco.

There were stories duct-taped to the cowboy wallpaper about what really happened on Sept. 11, and at Sandy Hook, the Boston Marathon.

He'd written about aliens and alien spaceships not that far from here. He'd seen a glimpse of something one night.

He'd written about the Unabomber being a CIA or FBI plant, and also Manson.

He'd written a long time ago about the fake moon landings and the death of Paul McCartney and why serial killers used to be so much around and now they are not and now it's terrorists it seems.

A dusty VFW coffee cup, white with flag, sat on the big wooden desk, next to one that said "DAD," with a red painted lipstick smack part of the design.

He recalled the Halloween with a good chunk of the local kids dressed up like little aliens and quite a few dressed up like Billy Lee Blueberry.

He thought it funny but his wife couldn't stand it. She took the kids and moved three blocks away, and now all of them lived in Dallas.

His sports photography awards sat behind him on a desk. He didn't look. He knew where they were.

He'd put them there himself.

Billy Lee got up. He stretched, took his coffee cup up to the front desk and walked behind the counter, entering not without fear the domain of Willhemina Sandy.

Billy Lee wasn't sure when they had stopped talking.

There just wasn't that much, or anything, to say anymore, but she made good coffee and she didn't seem to mind if he took some.

There was Billy Lee and Willhemina and in the printing room Buster, Rory, Pike, Clive, Juan and the others that remained at The Juno Sun.

The Sun was a part of a chain of papers owned by a few people in El Paso, maybe Fort Worth, Abilene.

They seemed to have been forgotten out here in the cosmos.

Neptune, Mars, Juno, Big Spring, Orion, Atlas all in the Constellation High School Football Conference.

Juno was the cement capitol of the world, some said, a while back. And Judge Roy Bean passed through here on his way somewhere else.

Commanches once ruled the land.

And the "there-there" was at times the Chinese, the railroad, the Gateway to the Pecos.

According to legend, just as it said on Wikipedia, a popular restaurant in the town served only beans. When asked what was on the menu, the reply would be "you know," which sounded like "Juno."

The world's biggest spur sat next to the road, a branch off Highway 20, on the eastern end. "The widest main street in the continental U.S.A."

"Oil, natural gas, prostitution," more of the Internet depiction of the area.

Under "famous persons":

Barrett Barnes, three-time mayor, fire chief.

A shark tooth found south of town sits in a glass case in the "museum" section of The Chuckwagon Café.

And so, Billy Lee Blueberry was going to kill himself.

Willhemina knew it, so did Buster, Rory, Pike, Clive, Juan and probably the others.

The whole town knew it.

There was nothing else to do.

It was what all writers do who run out of things to write about.

There was a chapter about it in all the journalism books, Blueberry had told his readers, so they knew.

Since he'd gotten the gift he couldn't refuse inside the old car.

It was a classic, a classic west Texas, what, what have you, a classic sign, a paradigm, motif.

Nah, that's not the word.

Maybe Willhemina and Buster, Rory, Pike, Clive, Juan and the others, the whole town probably, wondered about this new novel Billy Lee Blueberry was going to try to write and maybe that would take care of his writing habit and he wouldn't shoot himself.

Not today.

Maybe he would write a really, well, maybe his novel would suck and he would eventually kill himself, but maybe not today.

He would become another ghost haunting the town. There were many, oil workers, Chinese, prostitutes, gunslingers, swinging doors, cold air around a corner, crying in the night.

On the floor, against the wall, lay an old hat rack he needed to put back up some day, a string of white cowboy hats with dusty cards in the band: "News, "Sports," "Aleins."

Billy Lee grabbed his jean jacket from the wall.

He rubbed his hand inside the pocket.

"Peanuts, peanuts, peanuts, please be peanuts, not gravel," he said.

Willhemina did not look.

He grabbed the peanuts, picking out the whole ones and flipping the shells to the floor with the others.

"It looks good," he said, holding up Page One.

"Dead kids," said Willhemina without looking.

They had argued, silently, vehemently, about whether Billy Lee's story about how Bigfoots seem to exhibit an autistic "savant-ness," a key to their success, or the story of the carload of local high school seniors, out drinking, hit a light pole, all electrified, last weekend.

Billy Lee Blueberry stood behind Willhemina seated at her desk inside the horseshoe of the front office counter. The day after the paper came out was a day of relaxation, self congratulation or flagellation, time to sit in the coffee shop and take what's coming.

Billy stared out the front window at "the widest mainstreet in the continental U.S.A."

He'd been banned from the café, from church, the VFW, his home.

Not that you could prove, but that you could show, if there was someone who wanted to know, and if that someone was someone who had also been banned, otherwise they would not understand at all.

He'd been doing this all for ... he fired out his fingers to count the decades and his fist became a hand gun ... an awful long time.

How does that happen?

He scuffed around to stand at the front door looking between a VFW dance poster and a rodeo flyer out at the old car tied to the hitching post loosely.

He mumbled something about getting some air and went to sit on the front porch on the wood bench.

He sat down with a sigh, both he and the bench.

The winter sun ball clocked him at just about the eyes, sitting on top of the stores across the street, but it did not hit hard.

A sudden whirl of wind began to throw things about and then decided to dance in the middle of the street for just a bit.

The tiny eyes of the people across the street made the widest main street seem like a canyon.

He gritted a smile and reached to rub Cassius Clay's big head and droopy ears as he worked to get up, wag his little tail and get within range, then plop down, letting his jowls cover Billy Lee's boots.

Sometimes it's okay to just drift away without a big fuss. The thought came into Billy Lee's head. Like an Eskimo on a piece of ice. Maybe wave to one person standing there or not. Sometimes it's probably just time to stop shouting, and then stop talking and just let people alone, let them live their lives.

Even though you have no idea how they could live it without you.

When Cassius Clay had time to give you direct eye contact, the jowls, the nose, the eyes, the teeth that were just as likely gripping a soggy cigar a minute ago, reminded Billy Lee of the only editor he ever really loved. The intelligent tilt of the head that said, oh, well, it probably had said a lot then, but all Billy Lee remembered now was that there was this guy and that's how he looked, and it was a good memory.

Billy Lee saw that Cassius Clay, he was never just Cassius or just Clay, had recently pissed on the front right tire of the car by the pattern in the dust.

That's where it was left so many ... ummm, ago, with the leather reins from under the hood wrapped loosely around the hitching post.

The long '59 Chevy, off-green with wings, good tires, "from a friend," written by finger in the dust on the hood.

Who or why he did not know.

The keys dangled in the ignition.

There was a package on the passenger side of the front bench seat.

Billy Lee knew what was in there, inside the shoe box wrapped in old Christmas paper — smiling snowmen gripping brooms — and a red bow. The green bow had fallen to the floorboard "years" ago.

He had looked.

He watched another cluster of folks walking slowly on the sidewalk across the street, watching him.

As if he were not quite real.

A jackelope.

Those aren't real.

No wait, there's one.

Watch it.

The conspiracies – he had all of that.

They were the only stories he had ever been interested in, the only ones that made any sense to him to be interested in.

Sure, he wrote the obituaries. Sure, he wrote the football, city council, school board, and basketball stories, seventh grade, sixth grade, high school, and the cheerleading stories, the parade stories, the "98 Years Young!" stories.

He had to.

But, c'mon, c'mon!

Who Killed JFK.

The real Zapruder Film would show the limo stopped. Stopped! So they could make sure he was dead!

Who Killed RFK.

Powder marks by his ear. He was shot from behind, probably by a fake security guard.

Who Killed MLK.

The guy was actually tried and convicted, a civil trial, but nobody knows about it. Not James Earl Ray! That one guy, you know, c'mon! And there was a special forces sniper team. Read the transcript of the trial at the King Center website. Do it!

Paul Wellstone, c'mon the FBI was there almost before the plane crashed. He was going to stop the Iraq invasion. Cheney threatened him. He was up for re-election, he was going to win.

At Oklahoma City there were more bombs found inside the building. Ever hear of Terry Heaney, no, Yeakey, why was McVeigh driving away with no license plates? Why did he go to his death so agreeably, c'mon!

And at Waco you see fire shooting out the tanks. They burned those people alive on purpose, on television. And the same FBI sniper who killed Vicki Weaver is out there in the weeds picking off survivors.

On 9/11? What? Come ... on. Did that look like those buildings just falling down? They were exploding. Where is the plane at the Pentagon? Where the fuck is it? And the plane at Shanksville. Where the hell are those planes?

Nobody died at Sandy Hook or Boston.

Trust me. Why did they just leave those bodies inside the building and why did no parents storm that building. It was an act, all fake. And at Boston, fake blood, fake explosion, fake perps.

But why? I don't get it.

I just don't get it.

Of course I'm right.

Just do your homework, but why did they do it.

I just ... don't ... get ... it.

Aleins, which he seemed to always misspell, and alein spaceships not that far from here. Those were easy. Some people even believed him because they knew people who saw things.

The Unabomber being a CIA or FBI plant, and also Manson, to kill the '60s.

And it worked.

It always works, these guys are full-time, as Billy Lee used to say.

Paul McCartney and why serial killers used to be so much around and now they are not and now it's terrorists it seems.

And Patty Hearst?

The Symbionese Liberation Army?

Are you kidding me?

Who comes up with a name like that?

Some 20-some Special Agent with a Columbia education with too much time on his hands, that's who.

And Barack Obama?

In the age of Osama bin Laden?

And they got him elected with that name and they just laugh.

He knew who and how.

But never why.

Why do they do it?

Why do they want to ruin everything.

Why not do the good thing, the right thing.

"Truth can only be found on the most remote site on the Internet, the most dilapidated, under-funded, parents' basement, worst layout website there is."

Right?

"You're not interested in the truth. You only think you are. Your heart knows the real truth. Your brain does, but it's so far in there ... you only want to feel good about yourself. Feel okay about all that stuff, and somehow this 'search,' satisfies your deepest desires to not hate yourself and kill yourself, and even that would not end it. It still goes on. It does not end."

He'd heard that, too.

What he wanted to do was walk out into the desert and never come back. But he'd send notes, letters.

"I really liked when you came to our room and told us about being a news reporter."

The note from the kid was tacked to the wall, curled and yellowing.

The high school football team wore camo now, not so much like the early days when they all wanted to wear their hair long.

Cassius Clay hobbled down the front steps to go pee on another tire, so Billy Lee Blueberry pushed off the wood bench with all the names of anyone who had ever worked at the paper etched into the seat and back with the pocket knife that sat in a black coffee cup on Willhemina's desk.

Except his.

He'd always said there's time to do that.

"I'm too busy. I'll do it on the day I leave, how's that?"

He had said.

And now there was nobody askin'.

The door slapped behind him and Willhemina's face bobbed up like it was attached. Then she looked back down at whatever she was doing.

Billy Lee said, "Hello. Nice day out there."

He meant to.

He sure didn't feel old.

When he was walking around town in a hurry he felt just like he always did.

But lately he'd been taking more and more little trips into the cramped restroom off his office area.

Willie — he called her Willie in his head — probably thought he was having pro-strate problems, but he liked to look in the mirror. Because he could not believe what was in there. Sometimes he would just stare, and sometimes, like today right now he stood there over that little sink into that mirror that was the front of a medicine cabinet, and that he had to lean a little to look straight at it, and he touched the mirror with his hand, gently, like touching a painting, running a finger down the deep gulleys, fjords, inlets, like a living map, and it breathed and sweat, and sighed. It was alive.

He ran the water and flushed the toilet, ran a wet hand across the little hair mop hovering over his forehead and came on out.

He made a move to head to the back, stopped, did not.

He clogged back to his work "room," area, "office."

He stuck his hands flat and backwards into his back pockets in order to stare at the wall, pausing at another note:

Billy Lee was from here but he did not have an accent.

But he had noticed others and sometimes he liked to sprinkle that into his writing to show he had noticed.

Thank you, kindly. Pah [pie] Naht [night] faav. fah-ees. y'all.

He sat down at his chair, a stiff wooden one with curved arms. He pushed back and hoisted his feet to rest his boots there one on the other.

He had never sat that way in his whole life and guessed he wouldn't now.

Billy Lee brought his feet back down with a double stomp that must have made Willie jump.

He sat and stared, looked around a little, with his hands folded in his lap.

He guessed he didn't like what it had come to.

This was not easy, this sitting here and feeling all the years, like the first floor of a building with all the other floors having fallen and slumped in on his shoulders and him feeling every one.

Billy Lee Blueberry began his writing career in the typical way, feeling somehow surprisingly empowered, a burden lifted from his shoulders by the gift of writing, by pushing himself away from the common table, by raging against everything around him as a middle school student made the editor of the room newsletter by a teacher who might later have wondered what she had done — Joe McCarthy, U.S. quiz shows fixed, hula hoops, Sputnik, Rosa Parks, cigarettes.

In high school he wrote an editorial for the newspaper "If James Dean Had Lived."

It talked about everything he would have done, leading a righteous army of youth to crush the adult world, not because it was the adult world, but because it was wrong, and the young people were right.

Billy Lee Blueberry was nice, smiley, to those who had power over him. And to those who had no power over his life, well, they got the straight shot, whatever he was feeling at the time.

He observed that in himself as a young man, and he had sought to make amends.

He knew because he now held a crumpled note in his hands fished from his middle desk drawer to that effect.

Billy Lee could not recall ever having that thought and right this moment could not really tell how he had done in the effort.

Well, then.

Billy Lee pushed back his chair with a squeak and bent down because he knew it was there.

He set the box on the desk so he could push off with a hand to stand.

He walked to the front holding the Lone Star box with his Old Golds, three packs unopened, since he'd quit five years ago, DVDs, CDs, "Duck Soup," "High Noon," Mozart, "Blazing Saddles," Chopin, Beatles, two bullets, rolling back and forth.

* * *

Billy Lee stood holding his box at the front counter, overlooking Wilhemina, looking down at something she was working on.

"Well," he said.

"I guess."

Behind her on the wall, the Rockwell "Country Editor" took up most of the space.

He began to go and she said, "I got you something."

"For me?"

He put down his box and took the wrapped gift.

"You didn't have to," he said.

She looked up at him, her folded hands supporting her chin.

"Are we saving the paper?" he said and she didn't answer.

He took care with the tape, the bow, the paper.

He held up the pencil drawing, framed.

It was really very good.

"You did this?" he said and she placed her hands flat on the desk and nodded.

"It's really very good," he said.

She smiled, not showing her teeth.

The drawing showed a blacksmith, working in his shop, looking up as one of the new motor car goes by on the dirt main street, the driver and his lady passenger decked out in the finest motor clothes, goggles, special hat, gloves, a large, regal dog in the back seat, ears flowing.

"You came at a bad time," Willie said.

"There's nothing you could do, but you tried."

Billy Lee Blueberry made a cowpoke gesture with his finger to tip his cap and nod to Willie though he wore nothing on his head.

He clomped down the steps, looking up at the clouds, the wind blowing lottery tickets, Stetsons and burrito wrappers down main street.

He looked both ways for the special agents coming to take him out or take him away.

Nobody coming.

For a long time. Maybe not ever.

He didn't have time to wait.

Billy Lee put his box and Willie's gift in the dusty back seat and opened the driver's side for Cassius Clay. He crawled up and sat there just like granma in the Model T, like he knew just what he was doing.

Billy Lee Blueberry found the keys in the ashtray and started her up, sending up a smoke cloud, and backed ever so slowly into the street.

He saw silhouettes, like you make in kindergarten in the basement, the black face of you pasted on to a clay background, in the front window of the newspaper office, found first and moved on.

Billy Lee drove down the middle of the widest main street maybe anywhere, ten miles an hour, Cassius Clay sitting straight and proud and cocky like a dog playing poker holding a straight flush, like wait 'til the gang sees me now.

They stopped at the sign.

Looked right, left, front, behind, up, down.

Billy Lee turned the big wheel like a ship's captain, feeling the wind rocking the boat.

He headed out of town, past the café, past the assisted living facility, Target, the football field and the giant spur, and his own avenue, his the only little house on the street.

He lifted his foot from the gas for a moment, then continued on, approaching nine mph.

The wind whipped.

Gravel clanked into the metal.

At the end of town he looked to the side and saw into the whole lives of the Rogers family gathered on the front porch, smiling at each other then staring hard at him, except for a little girl standing on the cement front steps.

She waved to Billy Lee like someone on the curb in Dallas catching the eye of John Kennedy for a moment, with a sad look on her face like she knew what was coming.

Billy Lee flapped up a little wave of his own while keeping his knuckles white around the wheel.

In the rearview mirror he caught a glimpse of something that made him want to write a note to not lose that idea.

He let it go and it was gone, paper out the window.

And just as he passed the city limit sign the blowing gravel became snow, as if waiting for him behind a rock.

He drove on, slower, still moving.

Nobody coming, nobody behind.

The rolling, rocky desert stretched out like the arms of a tall man yawning.

He felt into the box, the gift left in the car all these ... ummm ... and the white-handled Colt revolver he knew would be there, with the elaborate etchings on the face and barrel like the arms and chest and back of a cholo.

He reached to the next box with his stuff, found one bullet and the other and worked to load them into the gun with one hand, not looking, while driving in the snow that was becoming a blizzard.

He stopped in the road, not pulling over.

Cassius Clay watched him fiddling with the gun and bullets — dropped one, got out, onto one knee to reach under the seat — nervous Billy Lee might cause an accident.

A break in the wind revealed an arrow-straight highway empty both ways for twenty miles.

Billy Lee climbed in, adjusted the mirror, looked in the right side mirror, now on the driver's side, got moving again.

The wind roared and whipped snow and tumbleweeds.

Now he could not see to drive.

He stopped again.

He inched, stopped, tried again.

Billy Lee felt the gun, looked over at Cassius Clay who was already looking at him.

The world was white and angry, perhaps confused having awakened in the nursing home and not knowing where it was.

Billy Lee stared straight ahead finding the trigger on the pearl-handled Colt as he saw movement ahead.

In the middle of the road, right down the dotted yellow.

Came a small man wearing a white shirt, jeans, tennis shoes, no hat.

Billy rolled the window down.

Jose?

Jose smiled, leaned down, spread his arms over the car like he was being frisked, to look inside.

"You like the gun?" he said.

"This is your car?" said Billy Lee.

"I thought it was meant for me, sorry."

"No, no, it is, it is, for you!"

"You like it? The gun?"

Billy Lee looked over and let the gun go.

"Yeah, I like it, it's nice. Nice gun."

Jose walked all around the car, the wind taking his black hair and the tails of his shirt, smiling, remembering.

At the window Billy Lee was waiting for him with his head out in the air.

"You wanna ride?"

"Where you goin?" said Jose.

"I don't know," said Billy Lee.

"I'm headed to town," said Jose.

Billy Lee looked in the rearview.

"Yeah, I guess," he said.

Jose went around, got in.

Cassius Clay gave just enough to let Jose sit.

Billy Lee drove off, slow, into the snow, looking for a road to turn around.

Jose sat silently, watching everything like he was on his first Caribbean cruise.

"Well, I guess," said Billy Lee as he turned the big wheel for a U-turn. Cassius Clay had to put one foot on Jose's leg to keep from tumbling.

"Why did you give me your car?" he asked just as soon as they got situated again on the road, inside the snowstorm.

"I knew you would need it some day.

"It looks like today, huh?"

Jose saw the gun and the one bullet sitting on an angle, stuck in the chamber.

"I left you the gun mostly. It was in the car.

"It was in Pancho Villa's band, my uncle, or my grandfather."

"Really!" said Billy Lee, looking at Jose and swerving as Cassius Clay and Jose put up paw and hand to correct the wheel.

"Perhaps, but ...," said Jose.

"I thought you might need it or at least write a story about it, see the white handle? It's unusual.

"Yes, I see."

"I drink some, see," said Jose, "and I give things away. I repent. I hear my mother's Jesus and I want to give all my things away and you know how it goes."

"Yep," said Billy Lee Blueberry.

Jose put up a pointer finger into the air as if he were the campaign manager for that particular pointer finger.

"I never take my things back. Never, not one.

"Only the cigarettes," he said.

"If you are not going to smoke them, you know."

He touched the unopened pack.

"Sure, go'head," said Billy Lee.

Jose watched the weather and petted Cassius Clay under his chin, then asked Billy Lee what had brought him to this day, and Billy Lee said it was things.

Also he had nothing else to write.

He had come to the end and so his life was over.

He just wasn't dead yet.

There were no more words left, but the movie kept playing.

They were not in sync.

Someone had made a mistake.

Time for the sad music, and soon even that should end.

He said all that in the time it took to drive the two hundred yards back to the city sign, welcoming them to Juno, Texas.

"Right here," said Jose, putting his hand on the door when they came to the big Target billboard.

Jose petted Cassius Clay, stuck his leg way out to reach into his pocket and dig out a little dog biscuit from his pocket. He held it until Cassius Clay chewed to the fingers.

"There's lots of dogs when I walk. If I feed them, you know, they are not as hungry for my ankles."

"Yep," said Billy Lee Blueberry, pulling to the side, getting two wheels onto the shoulder this time.

Jose got out, then crouched on his haunches, his arms resting in the window.

He brushed his hair back, rolled his sleeves to his elbows as the sun had begun to chase away the clouds and the snow.

"You got a lot on your mind," he said, looking straight into Billy Lee's eyes.

"Let me tell you this, senor."

He pushed his chest into the window and reached way in to ruffle Cassius Clay's head and ears. Cassius Clay growled in joyful play.

"It is all about you," said Jose.

"Everything is all about you, it always was and always will be.

"It matters what you think, what you write.

"It matters.

"You want to know why? Shit, I can tell you why, amigo.

"For a ride. Give me a ride to the front door and I'll tell you why."

"Yeah. Okay, yeah, get in, get in," said Billy Lee.

So Jose stood, opened the door, shoved in again and sat next to Cassius Clay, who looked at Billy Lee like what the hell? as Billy Lee Blueberry checked all his mirrors, put on his blinker, pulled onto the empty highway and turned immediately into the drive for the Target store.

He moved, so slowly, across the empty lot.

From behind you could see his blinker still on, and his head turned toward Jose, listening, looking every now and again to see where he was going, adjust his course, moving his head back and forth to see around Cassius Clay.

* * *

Willhemina looked up at the sound of tires rumbling over gravel, dirt, mud, blood, beer, probably at the corner, by the gas station.

Cassius Clay's ears and jowls flapped and tears smashed flat on his cheeks as he stuck his head out the window. The air stretched all the loose skin and he appeared to smile wide.

The big long car sped down the middle of the street, throwing up a wake of dust, hard gravel, rodeo posters, strollers, tiny children, and snow.

Billy Lee threw the big wheel and the big long car skidded like a hippie skier to a stop right at the hitching post.

The gun and the supplies box and all dived to the floor.

Leaving his door wide open, Billy Lee ran around the car, leaped the steps and saw that the front office screen was open.

If Willhemina had been right there he would have snatched her around the waist, bent her back and kissed her big, and told her he was finally home from the cattle drive and he was never leaving her again.

He saw the top of her head just above the front counter.

He ran around the corner to his desk, put on the white cowboy hat with the dusty "Alein" card in the band, that had been placed by his computer, threw back the shot of whiskey and poured another from the bottle.

He plopped down, threw away the beginning of the novel just as far as he could throw it and opened a new page.

By Billy Lee Bradbury.

He wrote.

"How did you know I was coming back!" he hollered, staring hard at his computer screen.

"Hey, Willie! Hey!"

He leaned back, way back in his chair and the chair raised on its hind legs, and he rode it, he raised his chin for distance, to continue hollering to Willie.

"How did you know I was coming back!"

Billy Lee Blueberry leaned farther, way back, holding the white "alein" cowboy hat in one hand, stretching up high, high as he could reach.

"It's Wednesday," she muttered.

* * *

Lirio Abbate
(Italy)

Now the Sicily correspondent of the weekly Espresso and the daily La Stampa after years of working for the Italian news agency ANSA, Lirio Abbate is an expert on organized crime, especially the Sicilian variety. After being the only journalist present at the arrest of Bernardo Provenzano, Cosa Nostra's "capo di tutti capi," in April 2006, he wrote a book the following year entitled I Complici (The Accomplices), about the close links between politicians and mafiosi. He has never been alone since then. He and his wife have a permanent police escort. But the death threats and his presence on Cosa Nostra's blacklist have not intimidated him. He still lives in Palermo and had another book published last year entitled Fimmine ribelli, about the "rebel women" who resist Calabria's feared 'Ndrangheta.

M. V. Kaanamylnathan
(Sri Lanka)

M. V. Kaanamylnathan had 50 years' tough experience in journalism and had worked for every Tamil-language newspaper in Sri Lanka when he took the helm of the main Tamil daily Uthayan in 1985, two years after the civil war flared up. Dozens of members of the paper's staff were among the conflict's 100,000 dead. Bombings, shootings, grenade attacks and murders were used to try to silence a voice that tried to keep to a middle course between the central government and the Tamil rebels. Five years after the official end of the conflict, Kaanamylnathan, who himself escaped an attack in 2001, and his newspaper are still making waves. Last year, a series of articles on land seizures by the Sri Lankan army was followed by a brutal attack on the paper's offices by six masked men.

Queirós Anastácio Chiluvia
(Angola)

Working illegally as a journalist was among the charges brought against Queirós Anastácio Chiluvia, news director of the opposition radio station Despertar, in February this year. It all began when the journalist went past a police station in a suburb of Luanda when he heard calls for help from detainees in the cells. Having tried unsuccessfully to obtain information from the police officers, he recorded the prisoners' calls and broadcast them on his station's airwaves. They were asking for medical assistance for a fellow prisoner who was dying of tuberculosis in an overcrowded cell. Chiluvia was immediately arrested and brought before a judge who gave him a six-month suspended sentence for defamation, offending the police and working illegally as a journalist. That is the price paid by a journalist in Angola for using the media to try to save a life. Chiluvia is still involved with Despertar radio, an essential counterweight in a country where freedom of speech can be easily denied.

Hanan Al-Mqawab
(Libya)

A 34-year-old Libyan woman from Benghazi, Hanan Al-Mqawab was forged in the fire of the revolution. Soon after the start of the uprising, she began working as a citizen-journalist for the Media Centre, an ad hoc organization created to cover events in the east of the country. She soon went on to work for radio Benghazi Mahali, presenting reports on the humanitarian situation, and then Shabab Libya FM, where she covered the situation of women and hosted a very popular programme called Isma'una (Listen to us), the first to talk openly about the abuses being committed by the militias. Its reports linking armed groups to egregious human rights violations led to a major demonstration on 21 September 2012 called "Save Benghazi." The resulting threats of death or abduction were too much even for Mqawab and her commitment to journalism and political activism. She finally fled abroad and continues to be a journalist in exile.

Yoani Sánchez
(Cuba)

A philologist by training, Yoani Sánchez is a celebrity in her own country and internationally. Time Magazine ranked her as one of the world's 100 most influential people in 2008. Her Generación Y blog, launched in 2007 with the aim of "helping to build a plural Cuba," covers the economic and social problems that ordinary Cubans constantly face. Like other bloggers, she has been subjected to varied insults (such as "contemptible parasites"), intermittent blocking and judicial harassment. In early 2014, she announced her intention to create an independent collective media platform in Cuba. "The worst could happen on the first day, but perhaps we will sow the first seeds of a free press in Cuba," she said.

Li Jianjun
(China)

For the past 10 years, Li Jianjun has been waging a battle against corruption in China. Li, 36, began working as an investigative journalist in his home province of Shanxi in the north of the country, where he exposed cases of corruption in the police. He was sacked in 2011 but didn't back down. Between 2012 and 2013, he took on the head of the state-owned conglomerate China Resources Holdings Co, Song Lin. Despite death threats and kidnap attempts, Li even took a minority shareholding in the company as part of his investigation. In April 2013, he highlighted irregularities in contracts signed between China Resources Holdings Co and three mining companies in Shanxi. "They must go down and go to jail," Li has said. "Only then could I feel safe, and I would be making a big service for public interests as well." Following an investigation by the Party's Central Commission for Discipline Inspection, Song Lin was removed from office on April 19 .

Johnny Bissakonou
(CAR)

The "ordinary citizen's spokesman" is how Johnny Bissakonou describes himself. Blogger, journalist, radio host, media editor – he has worn many caps during years of trying to provide as much information as possible about Central African Republic. His goal? To expose what's going on and work for a more democratic society. When the rebel Seleka coalition seized power in March 2012, he courageously reported its use of violence against civilians. This put him straight on to the Seleka blacklist and he finally fled the country after repeated threats and his brother's murder by militiamen who were looking for him. From exile, he continues to address the international population on his blog and by radio, hoping to be able to go back when his country is at peace again.

Ileana Alamilla
(Guatamala)

A lawyer by training and journalist by vocation, Ileana Alamilla fled Guatemala in 1979 and did not return until 1998, spending almost 20 years in exile in Costa Rica, Nicaragua, Salvador and Mexico. It was in exile in 1983 that she founded Cerigua (Centro de Reportes Informativos Sobre

Guatemala) to "break through Guatemala's international isolation and draw attention to the terror and crimes against its population." As such, she supported the 1996 peace accords that ended a 36-year civil war. She campaigns for the creation of a national system to protect journalists and, through Cerigua, has been condemning an unprecedented wave of violence against media personnel.

Dina Meza
(Honduras)

Presenter of the radio programme "Voces contra el Olvido" (Voices against Forgetting) and editor of the Defensores en Linea website, Dina Meza has been spied on, followed and threatened with violence and death almost without interruption for the past eight years, and had to flee abroad for several months in 2013. Her country is a living hell for journalists. Fourteen have been killed with complete impunity in the past ten years, 13 of them since the June 2009 coup d'état. Subjects such as human rights violations, mining or the "purge" of the police seem to result in automatic reprisals. Meza also covers the equally sensitive subject of agrarian conflicts. "Am I afraid?" she says. "My biggest problem is that I am afraid of doing nothing and my children need a different country."

Najiba Hamrouni
(Tunisia)

Najiba Hamrouni, acknowledged by her peers as a model of integrity, has spared no effort in defending the freedom of the press. Originally an ordinary member of the Association of Tunisian Journalists, she became the treasurer of the National Union of Tunisian Journalists, in 2008 and was elected its president in 2011. Her courage and [...]

Tshivis Tshivuadi
(DRC)

The secretary-general of Journalist in Danger, a local NGO, Tshivis Tshivuadi has worked tirelessly for freedom of information in Democratic Republic of Congo for more than 15 years. Instead of deterring him, his first death threats in 2006 just convinced him to keep going. He was threatened again on 1 September 2011 and branded as a government opponent but he coolly continued to defend the Congolese media's right to work freely. When M23 rebels threatened a journalist in October 2012, he loudly denounced this attempt at intimidation, to the point that M23's leaders issued an apology. On 3 May 2013, Journalist in Danger issued a loud appeal to "break the chains of censorship and self-censorship" – a bold message in a country where, despite superficial undertakings, journalists are constantly hounded.

Gorka Landáburu
(Spain)

On 15 May 2001, the journalist Gorka Landáburu received a package at his home in Zarauz, a town in Spain's northern Basque Country. It appeared to have been sent by a business association. When he opened it, 150 grams of Titadine, a compressed dynamite used in mining and by the Basque armed separatist group ETA for its bombs, exploded in his face. He will bear the marks for the rest of his life. In its communiqué claiming the attack, ETA called him a "txakurra de la pluma," meaning a dog in the service of the Spanish government. When those responsible were tried ten years later, Landáburu testified in court: "I am a journalist. You destroyed my hands. My left eye no longer sees anything. Scars cover my body. But you failed because you did not cut my tongue out." Long protected by bodyguards, he is now the editor of the Madrid-based news weekly Cambio 16.

Ali Anouzla
(Morocco)

The editor of the Arabic-language version of the news website Lakome, Ali Anouzla was arrested in September 2013 just for posting a link to the blog of a journalist with the Spanish daily El País that in turn had a link to a video in which Al-Qaeda in the Islamic Maghreb (AQIM) threatened Morocco. Although released after five weeks, he still faces up to 20 years in prison under Morocco's anti-terrorism law. One more judicial headache for a journalist who has specialized in criticizing King Mohammed and his regime. It was Anouzla who, in July 2013, revealed that a serial child rapist was among the 49 convicted Spaniards to get a royal pardon under an agreement with Spain's King Juan Carlos. He has also criticized King Mohammed's lavish spending and long absences, and the corruption among those around him. He says he is ready to pay the price of fighting against "the wall of fear."

Pham Chi Dung
(Vietnam)

Like others who have seen nomenklatura corruption up close, Pham Chi Dung returned his party card. Instead he devoted himself to writing and developing a critique of Vietnam's political class, which he knows inside out. He was a military officer for many years and was an aide to Truong Tan Sang in Ho Chin Minh City before Sang became president in 2011. He has written about public security and the dominant cultural, economic and religious ideology. He was arrested on charges of "conspiring to overthrow the government" and "anti-government propaganda" in July 2012 in connection with articles about corruption and the government's shortcomings, but the investigation was abandoned and he was released seven months later. His PhD in economics, his 11 books and his many interviews for the BBC, RFI and Radio Free Asia still do not protect him. His passport was confiscated as he was about to board a flight to Geneva in February 2014 to attend a conference on rights and freedoms in Vietnam.

Malick Ali Maiga
(Mali)

Malick Ali Maiga was a presenter for Adar Koima (Joy of the Hill), the last of the six radio stations in the northern city of Gao to keep going after the rebel MUJAO and MNLA groups took the city in March 2012 and repeatedly threatened its journalists. He drove around at night and saw these self-styled men of God committing abuses and trafficking in drugs. In May 2012, MNLA members gave him a severe beating and "advised" him to refer to Azawad ("liberated" northern Mali) in more positive terms. After residents helped to free him, he continued to provide news coverage for the city he loves so much "Gao is home for me (...) everyone there is my family." He was attacked again in August 2012, this time by MUJAO members, after reporting on the air that a protest had prevented the amputation of a youth's hand for theft. He was beaten with rifle butts for two hours and left unconscious outside Gao's hospital. After that, he finally fled to the safety of Bamako. But the Islamists did not weaken his resolve and he continues to work as a journalist in the capital.

Brankica Stanković
(Serbia)

It's not easy being an investigative journalist in the Balkans, as the Serbian journalist Brankica Stanković knows only too well. She has headed Insajder, the B92 media group's flagship investigative TV programme, since 2004. She was just doing her job in November 2009 when she tackled the sensitive issue of links between organized crime and hooligans that support the Belgrade football club Partizan. That may have been her last moment of complete freedom. Amid death threats and acts of intimidation that included the stabbing of an inflatable doll representing Stanković in the stands of the Partizan stadium, the police put her under protection. She nonetheless still continues to investigate organized crime and corruption.

Mabel Cáceres
(Peru)

Mabel Cáceres was already an experienced journalist when she launched the weekly El Buho (The Owl) in Arequipa, Peru's second largest city, in 2000. The stories she covers in detail include endemic corruption, illicit enrichment and the reconstruction of a regional "Fujimorist" apparatus (by the allies of former President Alberto Fujimori, who was sentenced in 2009 to 25 years in prison for murder, drug trafficking and other crimes). She has been the target of no fewer than 13 lawsuits in the past two years, which must be a record in Latin America. In spite of the protection provided by a Peruvian NGO, she keeps receiving frequent death threats.

Assen Yordanov
(Bulgaria)

The news website Bivol.bg(Buffalo) that Assen Yordanov founded with Atanas Chobanov in October 2010 quickly made a name for itself with exclusives about corruption, flaws in the judicial system and collusion between politicians and organized crime in Bulgaria. A few months later, it became the official WikiLeaks partner for the publication of leaked US diplomatic cables about Bulgaria and its Balkan neighbours. In the summer of 2011, Yordanov began organizing courses for local journalists on protecting communications against the phone tapping and hacking that is often practiced by the Bulgarian authorities. The site survives thanks to the enthusiasm of its journalists and to fundraising initiatives.

Advertisers obviously steer clear of it because they fear upsetting the powerful people targeted by its investigative reporting.

... 100 Information Heroes
Reporters Without Borders
http://heroes.rsf.org/en/

REBELLION

by Mike Palecek

F<small>ORWARD</small>

What I want is for every greasy grimy tramp to arm himself with a knife or a gun and stationing himself at the doorways of the rich shoot or stab them as they come out.

— Lucy Parsons

Custer died for your sins.   — Vine Deloria

Poverty is the parent of revolution and crime.   — Aristotle

Goodbye to my Juan, goodbye, Rosalita. Adios mis amigos, Jesus y Maria.

— Woody Guthrie

Any man or institution that tries to rob me of my dignity will lose.

— Nelson Mandela

It was patriotism that inspired me, not communism.

— Ho Chi Minh

In Peru a demonstration against a rise in bread prices is stopped because of threats to denounce those who demand bread as terrorists.

How greatly we fear language an electric cattle prod to drive us into corners where we cower for fear of being called terrorists or communists or criminals.

How did we allow those who don't give a damn about how we the 80 percent live or die to rob us of our language to intimidate us into cutting out our tongues and binding our limbs into lameness?

How can we be more afraid to be called terrorists than to die in the dark with no one there to speak for us?

— Marilyn Buck

I really do inhabit a system in which words are capable of shaking the entire structure of government, where words can prove mightier than ten military divisions.

— Vaclav Havel

The war ... was an unnecessary condition of affairs, and might have been avoided if forebearance and wisdom had been practiced on both sides.

— Robert E. Lee

I John Brown am now quite certain that the crimes of this guilty, land: will never be purged away; but with Blood. I had as I now think: vainly flattered myself that without very much bloodshed; it might be done.

— John Brown was hanged on December 2, 1859. Before he died, Brown issued these words in a note he handed to his jailer. Within one year, the first Southern state would secede from the Union.

http://www.civilwar.org/education/history/biographies/john-brown. html

The fight is never about grapes or lettuce. It is always about people.

— Cesar Chavez

Our revenge will be the laughter of our children.

— Bobby Sands

I began revolution with 82 men. If I had to do it again, I'd do it with 10 or 15 and absolute faith. It does not matter how small you are if you have faith and plan of action.

— Fidel Castro

We are sorry for the inconvenience, but this is a revolution.

— Subcommondante Marcos

PROLOGUE

The heart of liberalism is about compassion, dammit, it's not about campaign strategies.

— Joe Bageant

Attica! Attica! Attica!   — Sonny, *Dog Day Afternoon*

INTRODUCTION

A revolution is not a bed of roses. A revolution is a struggle between the future and the past.

— Fidel Castro

The first lesson a revolutionary must learn is that he is a doomed man.

— Huey Newton

As for ourselves, yes, we must be meek, bear injustice, malice, rash judgment. We must turn the other cheek, give up our cloak, go the extra mile.

— Dorothy Day

Chapter ONE

You never know what you'll do until you do what you do
When you're broke.

— *Todd Snider*

Well, the folks in town, they dress so fine
And spend their money free
They would hardly look at a factory hand

That dresses like you and me ...

Would you let them wear
Their watches fine
Let them wear their gems
And pearly strings

But when that day
Of judgment comes
They'll have to share
Their pretty things

— *Natalie Merchant, "Owensboro"*

A white man can't fight a guerilla warfare.
Guerilla action takes heart, takes nerve, and he doesn't
have that.
He's brave when he's got tanks. He's brave when he's got
planes.

He's brave when he's got bombs. He's brave when he got a whole lot of company along with him, but you take that little man from Africa and Asia, turn him loose in the woods with a blade, with a blade — that's all he needs, all he needs is a blade — and when the sun goes down and it's dark, it's even-steven.

— Malcom X

The old ladies, grandmothers, sit on the front porch, in rocking chairs. Three of them.

You see only their white heads, as they at least appear to be wholly intent on the work in their laps.

You are far enough away that if they pass gas you do not smell it, but close enough that you hear their voices. That is what caused you to stop in the first place, their murmuring like ghosts in the attic.

The porch railing is their end table, and on it sit flowered cups of something, pill containers, and a cigarette hanging over the edge, the smoke circling toward the porch ceiling.

There is no breeze. Somewhere a long ways away you sense children laughing.

You can hear them, the old women, a bit more clearly now. It is such a nice, bright spring morning. You hear birds tweeting when you stop your steps, your own thoughts, your endless filmstrip of your own worries.

You hear them talk to each other, the clicking of their tools, the clacking sound from somewhere, like one of those mystery sounds on the radio that if you guess what it is you win a free meal at the VFW, when one of them removes her upper without touching it and puts it back in.

"Most people suffer in silence," one of them says.

"Uh, huh."

"But you see it in their faces, their walk."

You stop to listen. They don't see you, aren't even looking.

You are late, but still you wait.

You are rewarded.

"Of course I always wanted to do what I was supposed to do," one of them says. Of course you can't tell which.

"Everyone have that in them."

"Ingrained."

"You want to do right.

"But after awhile some don't do that."

"Go outside it."

The house is white and so is the porch.

"See someone laughing?" one of the heads says.

"That is the goal of life. "

"Right there."

"Even while somebody else isn't laughing?"

"Cain't laugh?"

"Oww!!!

"Sheeet.

"Oww! Oww! Oww!

"Oh, man, ha, ha."

My Neighborhood.

My little sis' is inside the 'partment watchin Grover an' Elmo. She ain't even been outside yet, I don' know, but she don' know nothin' either.

That's good.

There's a little shit dog poopin, all squattin and shiverin. Them little dogs is the worse. There's a tree, a green tree, the only tree in that whole side of the block, an' there's the big dirt circle around the tree, and aroun' the tree is finger bones, and this big rope, an' you'd think it was a big dog, but then they let it out to poop and go tie it up an' it's jus' this little shit dog.

But don' go near it.

Unh-uh.

An' that ol brick 'partmen' buildin' what the shit dog come out of? Theys ol toys layin all over, an trash, an mud.

It's early mornin right now and I'm lookin outside cuz I already brush mah teeth an I gotta do my homework.

Ahm blowin smoke cuz my windows open jus a bit.

Ah got to get the am-bee-ants, the feelin what goes with the writin, the observin, is what my teacher says.

An ah kin hear the bus squeakin around an' the train, an' ah kin smell somebody smokin cigarettes, probly mom downstairs stickin her one foot out the door to keep her eye on lil sis.

Well, my teach'r tol me to speak clearly, not street talk, so ah'm tryin.

They are, they is, crossing guards jus' comin on duty, laughin. Lil sis' gets to be one a them someday. I already bin.

Ol' teacher she had us listen to this ol radio show where two boys from the ghetto went aroun to they neighborhood and talked to people to tell white people how they was livin. You know, put it on the radio.

An' then she was like, now you children go out and write about your neighborhood, observe, she say. And she wants us to write out our feelings, get 'em out, get out our anger, our fear, put it on paper, get rid of it, like trash. She say that writing can change things, that if people know the truth about how things are, things will change. She crazy.

Sometimes I be puttin' thangs in my writin, ya know, expanding a little here n' there, I don wanna my writin be jus lahk everyone else, ya know what ah'm sayin?

Ha, ha, well, like I say, theys a little shit dog poopin, shiverin and theys a big white guy crossin the street. He got on sun glasses and black gloves and black clothes and a beard and chains all down his leg runnin' up under his shirt.

He all bad early in the mornin'.

He be smokin and shiverin and waitin on the bus and shit, scraping the mud or poop off his black boots on the curb, lookin' up to not get runned over by the bus.

White people.

We not s'posed to make fun of anyone, jus' absberve, but good Lord.

White people at Wal-Mart? They look retarded, how can I be mad at them. They got they asses all hangin' out and they flappy arms and they clown clothes.

Raggedy Amercan flag on that tree, almos' fallin down, when it does that little shit dog will rip it to pieces just for somethin to do.

There are vacant lots that get growed over and trees are in there, and there was this thing that looked like carpet and went up to it and it was a dead dear, defrosting like chicken when the power out, the snow dissolvin' so now it was there and the carpet was fur and it was soft looking but the eyes were open dead and there were chunks out of the neck where the Thompsons or somepin' else got at it and my Lord how dead smells. They touched it!

Dead. Wow. Dead. Man ... dead.

But I think there are others, the really bad ones, not the clowns.

Oh, shet, oh, my, look at the time.

A bar with only one light left on the sign, harmonica music, teddy bears taped on a stop sign, the guy in a wheelchair with a sign sayin' he will work. Mud evey-fuckn-where. Lord.

Thas' 'nuff, for now, unless she makes us write more.

Ah'm not s'posed to do video games before school, but sometimes I sneak it anyway. I like seein' the heads 'splode, the white heads.

I don' like my neighborhood. I don' like my mom havin' to do the shet she do.

Ak'shly ... I bin a writer for a long time. I think ah'm gunna, going to quit. I need external validation. Of course, they say that insides should be enough. But it's not. I've went as far as I can with that fukn noise. It's meant to be looked at and if is not, well my hairy ass characters will keep on the lower class folks they always bin.

But, anyway.

See, theys my father and my grandfather, cousins, others in jail for "revolution." They kill somebody or steals something.

I'd say sometimes in writing, a writer is confused, like in winter, and then "clarity" hits like a icicle in the haid, like spring, and the simple truth hits you.

Teacher say something and 'bout a hunnerd years later I unnerstan'.

— write it the way that makes YOU feel good
— what if we treated animals like humans
— what if we treated prisoners like humans
— what if we treated humans like humans

She write that shit on the board and ah'm thinkin' she be gettin in trouble now from Mr. Hancock, an' ah'm lookin' at the door.

Ol' teacher be crazy, but it feel good to say these things. It do.

I was cleaning. It's a program. I take a bus and my job coach picks me up at schoo, work readiness they all calls it. I call it sumthin' else.

It was at a gym, a white fitness club, an' I clean, vacuum an' shit.

They was this ol' guy an' his ol' wife, park in front, on the curb, in a pickup truck.

He got on his red plaid earflap cap, sunglasses, red plaid coat, brown boots.

The ol' wife git him inside, on the bike, his boots inside the peddles, strap him in and he kinda rides it for awhile. Ah tries not to watch, but ah'm watchin.

He ride that bike, that ah can't never ride cuz I ain't no member, for about three, four minute, then the ol' wife, she pulls on his boots to get him outa there, an fetch his cane and hol' the dow fo him an' hol the truck dow and boost him up with a shoulder into the truck.

Thin she go off down the sidewalk, an' ah'm thinkin' where she goin to?

Well, the ol' guy pretty quick he got a cigarette stickin out his mouth, blowin smoke, sunglasses, cap pulled down, flickin' out the winda.

An' pretty quick ol' wifey she come up totin' a six-packa bottles, goes aroun' to the side, holds 'em up to him to inspect. He gives the ol' okay an' she puts the six-pack in a cooler in the back, an' off they go.

An' ahm thinkin' white folks, my Lord.

Well, in mah mind, mah thoughts, all I see is heads 'splodin' and shit. Ah got ten minutes 'fore I gottogo.

Ah'm on probation, see, an' they got these group sessions we have, has ... to go to.

You sit in a circle and close your eyes and let all your fuck'n worries all runs out down your arms to your hands onto the floor like poop, white folks be sayin' poop, and you stomp on 'em, and poop be flyin' everywhere.

Well, before we got doin' all this shit, they was this one boy over on the far side of the room, an' when the counselor was all tellin' us how it was goin' ta go for us in the next couple-a hours, it's OW! OW! OWW!

Somebody musta sat they chair leg right down on the top-a his foot, lettin' all they troubles out an' almos breakin his toes.

I laugh so hard, so hard almos puke, an I relaxed, closed mah eyes, thought about it being spring and all, remembrin' the "clarity" ol' teacher said about, and rememberin' back home, and how I got this gun.

Hello Northland.

And now The News.

Today, a prosecuting attorney was stabbed in the early morning outside his home and killed.

A judge died from a karate chop to the neck as he walked from his car in the parking ramp to his office.

A police officer's throat was sliced as he sat in his squad car and has since died.

And the CEO of a leading company was shot by a long range rifle as he was teeing off on No. 1 at 8:14 this morning.

And now, the sports.

And following the sports, the weather.

Here is a word from Fresh Of Breath Air Toothpaste.

The news was on the other night, it's always on.

I like to know what's happening.

"No honey, that's on the wrong foot."

I can't say that it bothers me.

My husband's in prison. And I know they're planning something. I say good for them. Somebody's got to do something.

And so, that's what I'm supposed to do.
My part.
I did it. Just like they trained me. It was good for something.
I got to go now.
"Honey, find your brother, we're leaving."

———————————

Behind the grandmas on the porch wall is a color photograph of '70s Beach Boys Jesus. There's also a stitched plaque, and a print of the old man with folded hands, bowed head, his daily bread.

"Passive aggressive, that's what you are."

"I know. I know."

"How so?"

"Aggressive aggressive, that's what I say, go for it, get 'em, right for the neck, the jugular, that's what mountain lions do on a goat."

"A goat."

"Jus' one goat."

"Did I stutter?"

"That child of yours ever get out the Laundromat las' Sat'day?"

"Oh, yes, thank you for asking. He puts all his shirts inside out so they come out right side, and thin if he has to, does it all agin. It takes time. My Lord, what a child. Who would think of that?"

"Like somebody said at church, the poor go to prison, the rich go to hell."

"Who said that?"

"All the other kids with the pumped up kicks."

"Better run better run."

"Faster than my bullet."

———————————

"Hola, como estas?"

Please sit down, let me tell you.

Have some beans, some frijoles, por favor.

We all live in this house, si.

And we are not going to work today.

We are going to another side of the city, donde nuestra familia ...

Here, take this, please sit.

Over there, next to the military base, they are planning to plow, to bulldoze, to demolish the neighborhood to expand the base.

They are going to plow over our neighborhood, like a field of weeds.

We are going to sit in the houses and not be moved.

Do you know of Rachel Corrie? The priest has talked about her. We know.

We are going to wear our uniforms to show we are working people.

And some are going to the Cathedral.

We will be in the houses, on the street with signs in Spanish and English, and in the church.

At the church we are going to ask the bishop to be on the side of the people, like Romero.

We will ask him, what did Jesus say about the military, so much money for the military, and so little for the people.

That is what we want to ask him, if he will hear us.

To do what, to kill people who won't come out of those houses, and everywhere.

All that costs money.

Jesus said don't kill. His father says don't kill. We are going to ask the bishop to say don't kill.

Here, please take this, sit down, rest.

We are not going yet.

Uh, huh.

Some have already died, more will die soon.

You know what I like?

The time right after lock-down, the end of another day, and that's when I get to mark it on my wall clock here with a big X.

This is the time when the noise starts to settle down and the danger. I'm a little less on-edge, but I don't really ever relax, even in my sleep.

I can't afford to.

And especially now.

It's taken a few years, but we finally got something goin' in about nine prisons around the country.

Starts tomorrow, right after chow.

I have a computer and a radio show, a podcast technically, I suppose.

The other guy does the technical, I do the writing. It's online, people can listen. I am way up here and the other guy is way down south.

We both don't know if anyone is listening. It makes us feel better, maybe someone is and maybe we are making a difference. I think we are, but I could be wrong. Maybe we are making no difference at all.

I keep looking for the FBI cars to pull up the driveway – winding, it's out in the woods. It's fun and we think it's the revolution, but we never hear from anyone.

The network says we have thousands of listeners, but we never hear from anyone.

We never get followed or shot at by the FBI. Nothing.

We just do the show, have our guests, our jokes, our commentary and music and all that and we are all happy, our celebration beer and peanuts or maybe beer and popcorn every Thursday, because we think we are doing something big, fighting the power, telling the truth.

Doing something. But maybe we're not. I don't know why the network would lie.

We probably have all those thousands of listeners, because why would they lie. But how can we be starting the revolution if nobody is trying to kill us or drive us off the road or sitting in a car on the street in front of our house all day? Is it because we are so tiny and nobody cares? Is that all there is to it?

We don't know.

We try not to think about it too much.

And look forward to Thursday.

Hey! Fuckhead!

Yeah you.

What the fuck you want?

What you doing here?

Theys twenty guns on you from all over the woods now, so you might 's well come on in to the campfire where I can see you good.

I bin waitin' to say that for nigh on twenty years, just like on Bonanza.

Come on, that's it, now sit.

Here take this, it'll take the chill off.

You're here because you're one-a them.

And you're here to come get me 'cause I know too damn much for my own good.

Well, you came on a good day.

I won't be here long.

Tomorra I'm lockin' up the cabin and headed in.

With my white hair and beard flowin' like John Brown!

Ha.

Two old white nigger lovers, yeah, I guess.

If that fire's a gittin' too hot, just move back a bit, mmm, hmm, lahk 'at.

You'll be wantin' my computer, like they do.

But they ain't no email, no dirty pitchers. You already know where I go on that thing.

Detroit. Chicago. Cleveland, Bronx, all that.

No where I'd go with my own gas, that ol' pickup.

Why they don't get jobs I don't know. Too much given to them, Communis fifth column.

But, my Lord.

If you've got a fucking computer and Google Earth, you can see with your own eyes, you don't, fucking forbid, have to actually go there, spend your precious money or time to actually check it out in person, but you can fucking see.

So, you're finally here.

Well, you better shoot me know because tomorra I attack.

I attack America.

Like Sitting Bull in a old red pickup two shotguns blazin' out both windas, radio blaring Johnny Cash full fucking blast.

Where's yer gun?

You ain't got no gun?

Who are you?

Nice boots they warm?

Do you fucking realize the difference in income in America?

Why?

Why don't people realize what people need?

Why do some got to be so goddamned greedy!

Health care, affordable wage, rent.

You think I'm crazy, right?

Does it matter?

Does it fucking matter what I am?

Mmm, these beans is good, over a far, sure you don' wan' none?

Thas it, just pull up, theys gooood.

It's jus' time, that's all.

Class war.

It's time.

Like some says, being born lower class in America makes some of us, probably most of us, class conscious for life.

You do not have power over your work, do not control when you work, how much you get paid, how fas' you work, or how long.

The workers was crushed b' thugs and money and prop'ganda.

You jus' work like a scared rabbit, afraid they're going to take the little baby carrots away, glad to be able to work for the little shit they spread out over the ground.

So fuck that all.

Do you know that your boss, if you work, I still don't know who the hell you are, makes about three hundred fuck'n times what you make. People just do not understand how much money is out there and how much they do not have in their hands for their families.

But I'm about to change all that.

Not tonight.

Tomorra.

Why me?

Why an old white guy?

Well, Mr. Fancy Boots, do you know that there are way fucking more poor white people in America than any other color? Blue, purple, maroon or fukn green?

More than all the jigaboos, porch monkeys, spearchuckers, jungle bunnies, coons, spades, spooks, tar babies and burrheads.

Way fucking more.

Did I stutter?

Because I know. I seen it all on the computer my son gave me for Chris'mas.

I know.

Now you know.

What you gonna do, han'cuff me or ride with me in the mornin'?

Huh?

Here, drink this, yer gonna need it.

Not all of it now, hey!

There.

You know fuckin' what?

You can think out here.

Not in the house.

Things change.

All the fuckin' stars, my man. And the smoke smell, the whiskey, cigarettes, the woods. It changes you the minute you're in it.

An' those twenty guns in the woods?

They are my people. My ancestors. Czechs on some big boat, others from Ireland, Norway.

And they all are fuckin' stupid as hell.

Because bad education, nobody they know knows anything, they think patriotic is good, don't trust others they don't know, but they trust the goverment to tell 'em where and when to go die, and they don' trust computers, but they do trust Barbara Bob at The News and Todd on TV because they have "official" positions and must know what's going on because they've been to college or at least somewhere besides here.

Well, fuck all that.

Drink up.

We are finding our horses.

Jimmy let them loose.

He wasn't s'pose to and now we have to round them up.

And we are going from Kyle, to the Knee, Manderson, Oglala, Pine Ridge and pick up where they left off, and riding to the Badlands, all the way to Rushmore.

We have guns, AKs, a Browning T-Bolt from the Rapid pawn shop, an old Hotchkiss in the back of a pickup, even bow and arrows, knives, Glocks, twelve-gauge,

We will ride in the night and burn.

We won't do like the blacks do and burn their own houses when we fight back.

That is so fucking stupid.

We burn white houses and white people.

We will have a few empty horses so they can ride with us, Sitting Bull, Geronimo, Russ, Dennis, Anna Mae, Jimmy Eagle, Pedro Bissonette.

Many will wear their U.S. Army clothes, which is confusing, yes, even to me.

But there you have it.

"I like the one who will just put everything into what he's doing," said the gramma in the middle.

"He shows faith in the bit.

"One hundred percent, win or lose.

"And see how cool that is when it works. Maybe 'spesh'ly a younger person.

"What does it look like when it doesn't work?

"Well, you do know Lilly's sister's boy?"

"Uh huh."

"Yeah, well."

"... I used to practice a harmonica, in the bathroom, real sof'. I think there would be such challenges of performing – that it would be something to encourage people to do that – things you don't think of.

"Well, how do I know? Things like how scared you get and how you do it anyhow, like that.

"To get on the stage, takes courage, there's other things like 'at."

"... Kids getting rich off sports."

"Who?"

"Nobody I know."

"They all think that."

"And when they don't?"

"Then what."

"... I see they askin' for firemens downtown."

"Uh-huh."

"I don' wanna be no fire man."

"... Mebbe a astronaut."

"Ha! You couldn' fit in no ass-tro-not costume!"

"Speak for yerself you ol' fool.

"Speak for yerself."

———————————————

There was ... well, she was actually on the board of Manhattan Eye, Ear and Throat Hospital, affiliated with Lenox Hill Hospital, between 2nd and 3rd Avenues.

Where the author of "How Dry Were My Hydrangeas" died of elective facial surgery at one time or another and the following month a Lucchese consigliere croaked during a facelift.

She was a woman actually, who because of things in her life had decided to give it all away.

Something about a soup kitchen, beggars in the subway had made its way into family oral history.

And of course her late husband cried out from St. Michael's, and her children howled, tore at their hair and ripped their clothes.

It's time, she said.

It is way past time.

It's all got to go.

All this stuff, all this crap.

How apropos, here it is.

My bible, under my fur coats.

I will sit for a while, I will take my time, because, irregardless, it all has a certain sentimental value.

You understand.

———————————————

Oh, well.

I'm going to do it anyway.

Write this.

Letter to the editor.

I know what everyone will say.

Think I'm crazy.

And then nobody will talk to me and I might lose my job, my family, lots of stuff.

Or nothing will happen.

And nobody will care.

They will just smile at each other and nod when I'm coming.

Or not even that.

Or way more than that.

And I know what will happen in ten years, twenty years, forty years.

I will get invited to the forty-year reunion and I won't want to go because I haven't talked to anyone or seen anyone for thirty-nine years and I won't know what to say. And I will be nervous about whether I should go or not and I'll go back and forth in my mind for five months before I decide whether to go or not.

And I won't go.

Because that tugboat sailed a long, long time, ago, hit a rock and sank to the bottom of the bay while nobody was watching.

And I will feel sad and confused.

Not satisfied.

And then when I am tracked down and found by the FBI and CIA by secret tracking devices because I am so dangerous, and so good, and so special, they will drag, no, walk me proudly, as angels and high school bands play.

And then when I get into court the judge and the lawyers will scream like in Hitler's court all the bad (good?) things I have done.

And people will cry, and just as in my dreams where I am flying over the town (nobody else can fly) in my underpants, everyone will know.

... She was the most beautiful. I watched her and she was a small-town goddess.

She's on Facebook now. I'm cruising Facebook like I used to cruise "the main."

Geezuz God.

Oh my God, you saved me for some reason.

I am going to write this letter and send it and there goes my life, into this letter, but it is what I need to do.

But before it is printed, I still have the weekend.

I wonder what everybody's doing tonight.

Seeya.

I gotta go now.

———————————————

Old ladies sitting on a front porch.

Their hair is white and freshly coiffed.

You are still standing there and they haven't noticed you. Maybe you are already dead?

Just sayin'.

"Perception is reality."

You hear that, but what does it mean? You wish they would speak louder, but with their heads down working they are really only talking loud enough for each other.

Need to know basis.

One is knitting a sweater for the neighbor baby, one a cross, and one a noose.

"Mother always told me, now honey, when you know you are going out, make sure you wear clean drawers because you want to present the best image in case you have to be picked up by the ambulance squad.

I'm shitting myself.

Of course you are.

Conclusion

Our apologies, good friends
for the fracture of good order
the burning of paper
instead of children
the angering of the orderlies
in the front parlor of the charnel house
We could not
so help us God
do otherwise
For we are sick at heart our hearts give us no rest for thinking of the
Land of Burning Children
                    — Dan Berrigan, part of statement at trial for Catonsville 9

On May 17th, 1968, Nine people, including Father Daniel Berrigan
and his brother Father Phillip Berrigan (David Darst, John Hogan, Tom
Lewis, Margie Melville, Tom Melville, Mary Moylan, George Mische)
entered a draft board and removed draft files of those who were about
to be sent to Viet Nam.

They took these files outside and burned them with home-made
napalm, a weapon commonly used on civilians by the U.S. forces.

They then awaited their arrest by authorities.

No privileged group in history has ever given up anything without
some kind of blood sacrifice, something.
                    — Bob Moses, Student Non-Violent Coordinating Committee

Why do we need to be pardoned?
What are we to be pardoned for?
For not dying of hunger?
For not accepting humbly the historic burden of disdain and
abandonment?
For having risen up in arms after we found all other paths closed?
For not heeding the Chiapas penal code, one of the most absurd and
repressive in history? For showing the rest of the country and the whole

world that human dignity still exists even among the world's poorest peoples? For having made careful preparations before we began our uprising?

For bringing guns to battle instead of bows and arrows? For being Mexicans? For being mainly indigenous? For calling on the Mexican people to fight by whatever means possible for what belongs to them? For fighting for liberty, democracy and justice?

For not following the example of previous guerrilla armies? For refusing to surrender? For refusing to sell ourselves out? Who should we ask for pardon, and who can grant it? Those who for many years glutted themselves at a table of plenty while we sat with death so often, we finally stopped fearing it? Those who filled our pockets and our souls with empty promises and words? Or should we ask pardon from the dead, our dead, who died "natural" deaths of "natural causes" like measles, whooping cough, break-bone fever, cholera, typhus, mononucleosis, tetanus, pneumonia, malaria and other lovely gastrointestinal and pulmonary diseases?

Our dead, so very dead, so democratically dead from sorrow because no one did anything, because the dead, our dead, went just like that, with no one keeping count with no one saying, "Enough!" which would at least have granted some meaning to their deaths, a meaning no one ever sought for them, the dead of all times, who are now dying once again, but now in order to live?

Should we ask pardon from those who deny us the right and capacity to govern ourselves? From those who don't respect our customs and our culture and who ask us for identification papers and obedience to a law whose existence and moral basis we don't accept? From those who oppress us, torture us, assassinate us, disappear us from the grave "crime" of wanting a piece of land, not too big and not too small, but just a simple piece of land on which we can grow something to fill our stomachs?

Who should ask for pardon, and who can grant it?"

— Subcommandante Marcos

If we must die, we die defending our rights.   — Sitting Bull

The tree of liberty must be refreshed from time to time with the blood of patriots and tyrants. It is its natural manure.

— Thomas Jefferson

A revolution is impossible without a revolutionary situation; furthermore not every revolutionary situation leads to revolution.
— Vladimir Lenin

People have only as much liberty as they have the intelligence to want and the courage to take.
— Emma Goldman

The end may justify the means as long as there is something to justify the end.
— Leon Trotsky

"Our strategy should be not only to confront empire, but to lay siege to it. To deprive it of oxygen. To shame it. To mock it. With our art, our music, our literature, our stubbornness, our joy, our brilliance, our sheer relentlessness – and our ability to tell our own stories. Stories that are different from the ones we're being brainwashed to believe.
— Arundhati Roy

"You said, 'They're harmless dreamers and they're loved by the people.' 'What,' I asked you, 'is harmless about a dreamer, and what,' I asked you, 'is harmless about the love of the people? Revolution only needs good dreamers who remember their dreams."
— Tennessee Williams

It is better to die on your feet than to live on your knees."
— Emiliano Zapata

"The only way to support a revolution is to make your own."
— Abbie Hoffman

Our masters have not heard the people's voice for generations, Evey, and it is much, much louder than they care to remember."
— Alan Moore, *V for Vendetta*

"Without Revolutionary theory, there can be no Revolutionary Movement."

— Vladimir Ilich Lenin

A revolution is coming – a revolution which will be peaceful if we are wise enough; compassionate if we care enough; successful if we are fortunate enough – but a revolution which is coming whether we will it or not. We can affect its character; we cannot alter its inevitability.

— Robert F. Kennedy

A revolution is not a dinner party, or writing an essay, or painting a picture, or doing embroidery; it cannot be so refined, so leisurely and gentle, so temperate, kind, courteous, restrained and magnanimous. A revolution is an insurrection, an act of violence by which one class overthrows another.

— Mao Tse-tung

Enjolras, pierced by eight bullets, remained backed up against the wall is if the bullets had nailed him there. Except that his head was tilted. Grantaire, struck down, collapsed at his feet.

— Victor Hugo, *Les Misérables*

Unjust laws exist: shall we be content to obey them, or shall we endeavor to amend them, and obey them until we have succeeded, or shall we transgress them at once?

— Henry David Thoreau

With the single exception of the American Revolution, the aftermath of all revolutions from 1789 on only worsened the human condition.

— Arnold Beichman

Let us be today's Christians. Let us not take fright at the boldness of today's church. With Christ's light let us illuminate even the most hideous caverns of the human person: torture, jail, plunder, want, chronic illness. The oppressed must be saved, not with a revolutionary salvation, in mere human fashion, but with the holy revolution of the Son of Man, who dies on the cross to cleanse God's image, which is soiled in today's humanity, a humanity so enslaved, so selfish, so sinful.

— Oscar A. Romero

Revolutions spring not from accident, but from necessity. A revolution is a return from the factitious to the real. It takes place because it must.

— Victor Hugo, *Les Misérables*

EPILOGUE

Free the prisoners, jail the judges
Free all prisoners everywhere
All they want is truth and justice
All they need is love and care
Attica State, Attica State
We're all mates with Attica State.

— *John Lennon*

You felt, in spite of all bureaucracy and inefficiency and party strife something that was like the feeling you expected to have and did not have when you made your first communion. It was a feeling of consecration to a duty toward all of the oppressed of the world which would be as difficult and embarrassing to speak about as religious experience and yet it was as authentic as the feeling you had when you heard Bach, or stood in Chartres Cathedral or the Cathedral at León and saw the light coming through the great windows; or when you saw Mantegna and Greco and Brueghel in the Prado.

It gave you a part in something that you could believe in wholly and completely and in which you felt an absolute brotherhood with the others who were engaged in it. It was something that you had never known before but that you had experienced now and you gave such importance to it and the reasons for it that your own death seemed of complete unimportance; only a thing to be avoided because it would interfere with the performance of your duty. But the best thing was that there was something you could do about this feeling and this necessity too.

You could fight.

— Ernest Hemingway, *For Whom the Bell Tolls*

I have always thought that in revolutions, especially democratic revolutions, madmen, not those so called by courtesy, but genuine madmen, have played a very considerable political part. One thing is certain, and that is that a condition of semi-madness is not unbecoming at such times, and often even leads to success.
— Alexis de Tocqueville, *Recollections on the French Revolution*

Revolution does have to be violent precisely because the Pharaoh won't let you go. If the Pharaoh would let you go, the revolution won't have to be violent.
— Michael Hardt

Look rather at the teachings of history, true history, not the history written by Party hacks: genuine democracy, the only valid democracy, is nourished with the blood of martyrs and with the blood of tyrants.
— Wei Jingsheng

Settle your quarrels, come together, understand the reality of our situation, understand that fascism is already here, that people are dying who could be saved, that generations more will die or live poor butchered half-lives if you fail to act. Do what must be done, discover your humanity and your love in revolution. Pass on the torch. Join us, give up your life for the people.

... Then there are those who resist and rebel but do not know what, who, why, or how exactly they should go about this. They are aware but confused. They are the least fortunate, for they end where I have ended. By using half measures and failing dismally to effect any real improvement in their condition, they fall victim to the full fury and might of the system's repressive agencies. Believe me, every dirty trick of deception and brutality is employed without shame, without honor, without humanity, without reservation to either convert or destroy a rebellious arm. ... Maybe when you remember this ten or twenty years from now you'll comprehend. I don't think of life in the same sense that you or most black men of your generation think of it, it is not important to me how long I live, I think only of how I live, how well, how nobly. We think if we are to be men again we must stop working for nothing, competing against each other for the little they allow us to possess, stop selling our women or allowing them to be used and handled against their will, stop letting our children be educated by the barbarian, using their language, dress, and customs, and most assuredly stop turning our cheeks.

... If you could see and talk to some of the blacks I meet in here you would immediately understand what I mean, and see that I'm right. They are all average, all with the same backgrounds, and in for the same thing, some form of food getting.

About 70 to 80 percent of all crime in the U.S. is perpetrated by blacks, "the sole reason for this is that 98 percent of our number live below the poverty level in bitter and abject misery"! You must take off your rose-colored glasses and stop pretending. We have suffered an unmitigated wrong!

How do you think I felt when I saw you come home each day a little more depressed than the day before? How do you think I felt when I looked in your face and saw the clouds forming, when I saw you look around and see your best efforts go for nothing — nothing. I can count the times on my hands that you managed to work up a smile.

— George Jackson

In Latin America, the bearded men who took to the hills in the early sixties were still there in the late sixties, but they had advanced no farther. They controlled mountain tops; the governments against which they fought still controlled the nations; no cities had been encircled ... unable to take over the country from the countryside, the guerillas of Latin America and Asia are now devoting more attention to the struggle in the cities. ... in recent years, guerillas have battled government forces in the cities of Algiers, Amman, Belfast, Calcutta, Caracas, Dacca, Guatemala, Montevideo, Quebec, and Sao Paulo. Other cities throughout the world have experienced milder forms of violence while some, like Santo Domingo and Paris, have been the scenes of full-scale urban uprisings.

No great theorist of urban guerilla warfare has yet appeared. There is no Mao of the city. Carlos Marighella, the leader of an urban guerilla group in Brazil, wrote a manual for urban guerillas, but his death in a gunfight with Brazilian police prevented him from demonstrating that the principles he described would work. Urban guerillas can offer few successes to be emulated by other urban guerillas. They have not taken and held a single city; they have not overthrown a single government. Urban guerilla warfare has not yet been shown to be an alternate means of seizing power. In the absence of any renowned living strategist of urban guerilla warfare or case study of a successful takeover, I have tried myself to distill from a variety of experiences and accounts a strategy by which urban guerillas might take over a city. The struggle could take place in five stages: the violent propaganda stage, the organizational growth stage, the guerilla offensive, mobilization of the masses, and the urban uprising. Each stage is marked by different objectives, targets, and tactics.

(... in conclusion, pg. 18)
... To fight in the cities, guerillas must develop an urban strategy. What I have described from the guerillas' point of view is of course a textbook model. It assumes organizational development and a single-mindedness to pursue their objectives that is not yet apparent in existing urban guerilla groups. Some individual, or some group, must develop a practical doctrine and demonstrate that it can be implemented successfully. In the coming decade, the action is likely to be in the cities. We must not overlook both the possibilities and the potential threat raised by urban guerilla warfare.
        — Brian Michael Jenkins, "The Five Stages of Urban Guerilla Warfare: Challenge of the 1970s," July 1971, The Rand Corporation

The urban guerrilla is a person who fights the military dictatorship with weapons, using unconventional methods. A revolutionary and an ardent patriot, he is a fighter for his country's liberation, a friend of the people and of freedom. The area in which the urban guerrilla operates is in the large Brazilian cities. There are also criminals or outlaws who work in the big cities. Many times, actions by criminals are taken to be actions by urban guerrillas.

The urban guerrilla, however, differs radically from the criminal. The criminal benefits personally from his actions, and attacks indiscriminately without distinguishing between the exploiters and the exploited, which is why there are so many ordinary people among his victims. The urban guerrilla follows a political goal, and only attacks the government, the big businesses and the foreign imperialists.

Another element just as harmful to the guerrillas as the criminal, and also operating in the urban area, is the counterrevolutionary, who creates confusion, robs banks, throws bombs, kidnaps, assassinates, and commits the worst crimes imaginable against urban guerrillas, revolutionary priests, students, and citizens who oppose tyranny and seek liberty.

The urban guerrilla is an implacable enemy of the regime, and systematically inflicts damage on the authorities and on the people who dominate the country and exercise power. The primary task of the urban guerrilla is to distract, to wear down, to demoralize the military regime and its repressive forces, and also to attack and destroy the wealth and property of the foreign managers and the Brazilian upper class.

The urban guerrilla is not afraid to dismantle and destroy the present Brazilian economic, political and social system, for his aim is to aid the rural guerrillas and to help in the creation of a totally new and revolutionary social and political structure, with the armed population in power.

— Carlos Marighella, *Mini-manual of the Urban Guerilla*

We have the techniques, the resources, to get rid of poverty. The real question is if we have the will.

— Martin Luther King Jr.

The young generation don't want to hear anything about the odds are against us. What do we care about odds? ...

When this country here was first being founded there were 13 colonies. The whites were colonized. They were fed up with this taxation without representation, so some of them stood up and said "liberty or death." Though I went to a white school over here in Mason, Michigan, the white man made the mistake of letting me read his history books. He made the mistake of teaching me that Patrick Henry was a patriot, and George Washington, wasn't nothing non-violent about old Pat or George Washington.

— Malcolm X

In the final analysis, poverty means death: lack of food and housing, the inability to attend properly to health and education needs, the exploitation of workers, permanent unemployment, the lack of respect for one's human dignity, and unjust limitations placed on personal freedom in the areas of self-expression, politics, and religion.

— Gustavo Gutierrez, *A Theology of Liberation*

(End Notes)

— Table of Contents, "Scanlan's Monthly," January 1971

Scanlan's Monthly was a short-lived monthly publication, which ran from March 1970 to January 1971. Edited by Warren Hinckle III and Sidney Zion, it featured politically controversial muckraking and was ultimately subject to an investigation by the FBI during the Nixon administration. It was boycotted by printers as "un-American" by 1971. According to the publishers more than 50 printers refused to handle the January 1971 special issue Guerilla War in the USA because it appeared to be promoting domestic terrorism. The issue was finally printed in Quebec and in a German translation in Stuttgart (Guerilla-Krieg in USA, Deutsche Verlagsanstalt 1971).

Scanlan's is best-remembered for featuring several articles by Hunter S. Thompson, and especially for what is considered the first instance of gonzo journalism, Thompson's "The Kentucky Derby Is Decadent and Depraved". Thompson's articles from this period are collected with others in The Great Shark Hunt.

In the magazine, its name was described as being that of a "universally despised Irish pig farmer".

The "Guerrilla Issue" also included a picture of President Nixon having lunch with a group of business men. The caption identified each of the individuals and enumerated each one's alleged criminal record. This was the primary reason for the enmity that ensued in Washington. That particular issue was eventually printed by a small Quebec (Canada) company.

— Wikipedia

When I give food to the poor, they call me a saint. When I ask why the poor have no food, they call me a communist.

— Dom Helder Camara

Excerpts from Scanlan's Guerrilla War in the U.S.A., January 1971 Issue
  • War Memoirs of a Black Marine
  • War Memoirs of a White Marine
  • Interview with Father Daniel Berrigan
  • Interview with a Street-Fighting Woman

War Memoirs of a Black Marine
  I got back to the world on December 17, 1969.
  When I left 12 months before, I didn't know much about what was going on in Nam or anywhere.
  I learned a whole lot in Nam.
  A whole lot from the brothers, and a whole lot from the people.
  I was born in Georgia and grew up in Bedford-Stuyvesant. At home I'd been in a lot of trouble coming out of some fighting we'd been in on the block. I got into the Green Motherfucker, the Marine Corps, mostly to make my bird, cause it was getting hot on me. I hadn't been in no movement, but I had thrown some rocks at pigs.
  I didn't know much when I got over there. I had never met a real brother, you know. It started blowing my mind when I first got over there — brothers walk up to you and give you some power and you know they're friendly, not afraid of the pigs over there, they got themselves together. Man, I was never so glad to be black as I learned to be in the Nam.
  It was like an organization, you dig, but better than a big organization: it was a lot of little groups, ready and all moving together. Not into fighting each other. Into fighting for each other.
  We'd do a lot of dope. Smoke a number and get mellow, then rap

down about what was happening. We wondered if the movement back in the world would ever get together. A lot of talk about the Black Panther Party and about the Black P. Stone Nation.

We were trying to get all the brothers together, to build understanding — that takes extra heavy rapping, you dig, and your shit must stay together. The pigs, the beasts, keep fucking over you, constantly harass you, try and spy on you, rip off the heaviest dudes.

We had to deal with the problem, and we had to use force or violence when necessary. This is a thing that some people who are in an organization are afraid to use — their minds start to wondering about the penalties. But you had no choice, you got to survive, to build your thing, and the pigs are murdering. They don't stop, so you can't.

It was necessary to plot against the pigs in some areas. Just the same as here. The pigs are all around, and you got no alternative but to just do them, you know. Sometimes someone would just do a pig ... sometimes people got together and decided who had to be gotten. There isn't any point of doing things without an organization, you get a whole lot of people doing different things and somebody gets ripped off.

There were lots of CID (Criminal Investigation Division) cats, and lots of them died. Da Nang in September of 1969 is a good example. There was a black pig, a friendly dude, but his stories didn't all check and people got suspicious. We were pretty sure then, so we followed him to some area in Da Nang the pigs thought we didn't know about, and that proved it. So a bunch of the brothers started talking to the dude and asking him questions like why he was a pig and kept him moving, and later on he was just snuffed.

In July of 1969 I was in the Quang Tri area of I Corps. The problem there was communication. A bunch of us solved that problem by ripping off a couple of trucks and stuffing them with our people. We ran into a pair of brothers, Army brothers; we blew their minds. We rapped awhile and all of us went to their compound. It must have been 30 brothers by that time. We took over their mess hall, the Army brothers and us, not much talking, but we would give each other the power and raise the fist, you dig. People kept coming all night and we took over a hooch. It was mellow. Dudes were high, and high on black people. People kept coming in all night.

A lot of Army brothers were tankers. It was heavy the next day, because we down what a pig the colonel was who was CO of that unit. The pig was a racist and a fool. That morning he sent up some MP's to break up the party. They came around and hassled us. Brothers wouldn't even hear what they had to say, they knew who it was that time. Two of the brothers got quiet and slid when the shit started. Next thing anyone knew, this tank rolled up to the HQ hooch and it was brothers in it! This time we hit the colonel, 'cause he was in that hooch over there. It was a gas. Black MP's moved over to our side and we got our weapons and disarmed the white MP's.

There was a black captain; he had a pretty good reputation, but what he ended up doing was to negotiate for the colonel. His name was Sanders. They had sent out radio calls for assistance; we heard that from our radiomen. They had tried to jam them but it hadn't worked. So there was helicopters and things flying around. We negotiated and finally the Marine brothers retreated back to Quang Tri. Two days later the colonel, Jackson his name was, pulled open his desk drawer and this hand grenade blew him out all the windows at once.

It wasn't long after that that they tried to split us up. I got transferred to Da Nang, doing supply work. The brothers there were as together as in Quang Tri, and I got tight with a bunch of beaucoup heavy brothers. By September when the CID pig got offed, we thought that we had our area pretty well together. We knew most of the brothers and had them going in the right direction. Blew my mind when this little brother, one Thursday night in the hall, emptied a clip of an M-16 right into this lieutenant. I didn't hardly know the dude, but I knew that lieutenant for a pig. It didn't surprise me none that he got blown away, but the little brother who did it sure got fucked for it.

Most of the brothers knew that the NLF didn't consider them the enemy. In May of 1969 VC saved the life of Brother Pitts, a dude from Philly who was close to me. He had been point man on patrol, and someone signaled him with a whisper — like psst — to get down. He got down and shit started flying. When it was over he was the only one left alive, the others were all white dudes. He never shot at a Vietnamese, and, like all of us, he used to fuck up whatever equipment he could.

War Memoirs of a White Marine

I don't know why I joined the Marine Corps.

I guess I wanted something to do.

I had been working for a little less than a year at a General Motors parts warehouse in St. Louis, where I'm from. I couldn't see spending my life there, and I didn't know what else to do, so I joined. I guess I thought the same thing about the Nam. I heard you got less shit from the lifers in Vietnam and that's true. If lifers are too tough, someone just blows them away.

I really thought I'd made a mistake when I got to Da Nang. I had the job of air facility at the dump about a half mile from the base. Every morning about 9 o'clock I'd head for the dump. I'd start getting little kids and old women in the road about halfway there. Some of them had arms and legs missing and were really all fucked up. They'd just stand there, and you had to run them over or slow way down. Some of them would jump right on the truck with you and start going through the garbage.

I started dreaming about those kids. I still do. Fucked up kids, all ruined. A lot of people thought that I was crazy to worry about those kids, but they didn't have to see them every day. After about two months I thought I was going crazy, so I volunteered for combat. It wasn't hard because I was qualified as a radioman.

The thing about being in the Nam is that you are really alone at first. You see shit going down, but you don't know what's happening, and you don't know who you can trust. About my first day there I started doing dope a lot. It's good dope, and cheap. You can get really tight with people over dope. There was even a whole thing about dope and pigs — most officers were pretty cool about it; they would warn you when they thought you were fucked up too much and otherwise they'd leave you alone.

As radioman I saw a lot of action. I went on beaucoup patrol and saw a lot of asshole officers. Some really dumb motherfuckers. I was on patrol in Happy Valley in August of 1969, around the 21st, and we got led into a fucking trap by this incredible lieutenant. Christ, he was stupid. He got uptight and ordered us into the trees where I knew there was a lot of VC around. About an hour later there was only nine of us left. We got out, but it wasn't his fault.

About 15 minutes later he wanted us to go in again. The corporal just stood in front of him about four feet away and argued that the dude was insane. Then he didn't say another word; he just ripped off his whole clip into that fucker. It nearly cut him in half. Nobody said a word. Nobody ever did.

After that I started digging that you could trust people, and I got pretty tight with the dudes on that patrol and a lot of other cats. We made some friends in the little villa near the pass that goes over into Happy Valley and got to know a woman there. I really loved her. She knew some English and we walked about the war a lot. I think she was a VC. I used to bring her medical supplies at first, and lots of stuff. I got tight with corpsmen and could rip off lots of it.

I heard that some Army people in the South were wearing red scarves when they wanted to be neutral in the war. They said the VC didn't shoot at them when they all wore red scarves, just like they didn't shoot at brothers that much. So I got one. We all did. I don't know if it worked; we never saw too many VC. The captain threatened to shoot us all for treason for wearing the red scarves. He knew it was bullshit — if anybody was going to get shot it wasn't us. I stopped carrying ammunition after that. Didn't for the last three months in the country.

The more I found out about what was happening, the more I didn't know which side I was on. I couldn't fight the Vietnamese, but I couldn't see defecting the way a lot of people I heard about did. I wanted to come home, and I couldn't see shooting at my own people.

I went AWOL for a week and a half, but they found me in the villa.

The third night I was there I heard some noise outside and wanted to investigate, but my woman wouldn't let me — she went outside herself with three dudes, VC. I thought I'd had it.

We talked until daylight, drank that good green tea and talked. They were really interested in the demonstrations; they had heard of Berkeley and wanted to know how long it would be until we had a revolution there.

Later on in the Da Nang brig, we talked about the whole thing a lot. I was glad to be in the brig; I could talk there and I didn't have to decide what to do.

My tour ran until February, 1970, but they let me come home in December, because I just started refusing orders all the time and said that I would shoot anyone who tried to make me do anything.

I got an Undesirable Discharge.

I was lucky.

Interview with Father Daniel Berrigan

The Reverend Daniel J. Berrigan is the 49-year-old Jesuit priest who, with his brother and seven other Catholic war protesters, used handmade napalm to destroy draft records at the Selective Service Office in Catonsville, Maryland, on May 17, 1968.

How did your group plan the Customs House action?

The idea we had with the Customs House action was not to use blood that time, but to use napalm. Napalm was being used on children and women — not only in Vietnam, but all over Latin America — and we were selling it in Israel and throughout Africa. The horror was international and we thought it would be a very powerful symbol to destroy those files, those papers, those hunting licenses with the same material that was being used on human beings.

We had everybody's task thoroughly outlined. Then we made the napalm together. It was one part soap and two parts kerosene. Let me tell you, if you ever want to try something very good on material or property that has no right to exist, this is a terrific formula. It's totally incendiary, and it allows Americans to realize up close what the real product is like.

Through one of our friends, we found the wife of a Green Beret who had come home from Asia — she was very anti-war as a result of his experiences there. She read us the formula out of a Green Beret handbook ... read us the formula all the way from California. It was so simple, it just seemed to be a natural.

Now you're being sought by the FBI for refusing to go to jail. Yet when you performed the act at the draft board, you and your compatriots stood around and watched it burn until the police arrived. What is the difference in your attitude and thinking then and now?

That was the first really large draft board action. It was the first of the trials for this sort of thing, and we still had some hope that the trial might be a forum for political issues — that it might be possibly be an important factor in turning this thing around. Well, we did get the forum; we got hundreds and hundreds of people from all over the country and the tremendous night sessions and a very hot close-up trial with a lot of politics. But we were found guilty. We were disposed of. That made us think the thing through again.

The important thing to talk about, though, is not just the success or failure of the venture, but what it's leading to for the future. In the last year of draft board actions, every one of the groups involved has gotten away without an indictment. In this particular movement people are now doing their utmost to do as much damage as then can, and to get away with it.

You have talked about the possibilities of existing underground in a sense, surfacing from time to time and flaunting the FBI. What do you hope to accomplish?

What do I hope to accomplish? I still have a basic sense that good people can be brought further and that it's very important in every way possible to communicate with them. I prefer to do my writing rather than just expose myself through the mass media, but I'll do both for a while. What I most prefer is sitting down with small groups of people and talking about our lives, because that's the most basic revolution I know about and the area where we really get to one another — get our fears and terrors and dreads into the air and move closer to real adult views.

Now, a lot of the saboteurs underground would disagree with this entirely and say that it's merely playing their game again and has nothing to do with them.

I have a very great sense that there is going to be much more sabotage and that the government itself is inducing it.

Do you feel any hostility or resentment at any time? Does it lead to feeling that the masses are never going to move?

If I have anger in me, it's against our political leadership. It's very hard to keep a balance or even a charitable decent attitude toward these people or even a conviction that they are decent people. I find that harder as the days go by because I have a nightmarish feeling that their vision of man and the vision of history is so corrupted and so militarized and so anti-human that they're really going to bring the whole thing down. And that is a very defeatist kind of attitude to carry into my situation.

You know the students who were attacked in the streets of New York in March were in almost every instance unable to connect with any of these workers. The workers came at them with primitive arms and a kind of mob anger, so those kids were, practically speaking, wordless as well as defenseless.

But supposing there were circumstances where it was possible for a few students and a few working families to sit around on a regular basis.

For instance, I know of some Cornell SDS people who have actually moved to other cities and actually started communes in working class neighborhoods and have gone to work in factories and gotten ready for this kind of long haul that I am speaking of where you really are trying to get together with people whose lives are very different than yours, and whose personal, religious, social perceptions are giving way under their feet. They're being taxed out of existence. They're feeling the encroachment of middle age and no job advancement. They have brutish jobs that offer them no human recompense.

And then many of them are seeing their own children going through changes that they were never ready for. So it's no wonder that they work off the feeling of personal assault by going and assaulting others.

Where do you think the next few months will take you?

My mother is quite sick right now, and, according to my family, the FBI hangs out around the hospital in great numbers. They're like vultures around the dead, thinking that I would be foolish enough to appear.

It's part of their cowardice and part of their misunderstanding of real human feeling that they would even hang around a sick bed, a death scene, and take advantage of someone very old. But that's part of the cowardice by which they rule anyway.

Interview with a Street-Fighting Woman

What is street-fighting like?

The air is electric. You start runnin' down the street like a wild woman. Your body it feels really good — there's a group consciousness. You feel a People's Army. It's crazy 'cause all you have is rocks and bottles and maybe a few Molotovs, but you're fighting the pig and that's a rush.

Why do you go into the streets?

I go into the streets 'cause businessmen drink my wine. A couple of years ago I didn't know why I was there — I could define it. It was a gut reaction. But over the years my political consciousness has risen. Dig it, like I used to want to be Suzy Q. Remember her? You, know, Mick Jagger singing, "I like the way she walks, I like the way she talks ..."

What kind of actions were you in and where?

My favorite action was November, 1969, in Dupont Circle, Washington D.C. It was the night of the assault on the Vietnamese Embassy. I had a can of lighter fluid upside down in my jacket pocket with a nozzle through a hole I'd made for it. I could just put my hand in the pocket and squeeze the can — squirt! I had a religious-ecstatic visions of a flaming Vietnamese Embassy ... There were lots of little fires in Washington that night. I got a charge out of them. The pigs were really chasing us and blowing their stupid tear gas. At one point, when the wind changed, the pigs gassed themselves and we tore up Connecticut Avenue. We teased them all night. Sometimes they chased us, sometimes we chased them. And when the Mobilization marshals got creamed, everyone was happy — the people and the pigs.

Another time, when I was still at school, we staged a building takeover. It was this really fancy edifice — plush offices with leather furniture and silk wallpaper — but the school didn't have any money to let poor people in for free. That night my best girlfriend got beaten up by a pig, and we tore the place apart.

We went through files and secured classified government documents proving CIA-university complicity and the school's being just a training ground for rich men's kids. This was too much on top of the behind-the-scenes policy-making in southeast Asia by the fat cat professors who fancied themselves intellectuals (yecchh!) and upholders of democracy.

We smashed up their $1,200 mahogany desks and used them for barricades. Then we split all the leather couches and chairs and decorated the fold raw silk with revolutionary wall-painting. We scored tape recorders, typewriters, and various knick-knacks. Most important, though, was that a group with different ideologies, life-styles and backgrounds had got the together, maintained security and done what we set out to do.

We felt we could relax — why not celebrate?

So we sat around and blew two ounces of really good dope and ate peanut butter sandwiches.

We called up every newspaper in town and gave conflicting Yippee press statements. Our first demand was the immediate release of Sirhan Sirhan.

It was really funny how the news desk reacted. Of course, that was the whole idea. The old public still isn't hip enough to know who we are and what we want. We are everybody and we want everything and I don't think that's too much to ask.

Do you?

Do you think street-fighting has lost its effectiveness as a tactic?

Basically, what I gained out of street actions was a progressive feeling of coming together with my sisters and brothers. We never did smash the state like we set out to do, but the streets laid the foundations to make this possible. No matter what city I travel to, I see old faces.

People get together and stick together after the streets.

But no more street-fighting now after Kent State, etc.

Fuck the streets.

We are moving on to urban guerrilla warfare and a higher consciousness.

We learned to live is to love and to survive is to fight.

Our struggle is one of armed love, and there's nothing contradictory about it.

How did you avoid arrest in the streets?

We stayed in small cadres of four or five people. Whenever someone shouted "Tex," or some other code word, we regrouped.

We watched out for each other. We tried not to be too brash, just brash enough.

We studied our territories and knew alleyways.

We usually left rock piles at strategic points. B

ut fast running and good karma were our best defense.

Is there a culture connected with street-fighting? Which came first?

The culture came first, but it's developing because we're still developing.

The culture I identify with comes out of LSD and the whole hippie thing.

Love, sharing.

But the fact that most people are cold and hungry, while a few buy new fur coats and cars, negates the hippie as a stupid, selfish, bourgeois individual.

So flower children carry guns instead of flowers because that's the only way everybody's gonna eat, 'cause the businessman drinks your wine and isn't going to give that up.

And he sucks your blood and sends his dogs into the street to get you and then street-fighting saved up.

Witnesses said they could hear Lolita's voice above the commotion, and it was a shrill, chilling sound. "Viva Puerto Rico Libre!" Long live free Puerto Rico, she yelled as she and her compatriots unfurled a Puerto Rican flag and blasted away with Lugers and an automatic pistol.

Police found a handwritten note in her purse, alongside some lipstick and Bromo-Seltzer tablets: "Before God and the world, my blood claims for the independence of Puerto Rico. My life I give for the freedom of my country. This is a cry for victory in our struggle for independence ... The United States of America are betraying the sacred principles of mankind in their continuous subjugation of my country ... I take responsible for all."

— Lolita Lebron, one of four Puerto Rican nationalists who attacked the U.S. House of Representatives with semi-automatic pistols, March 1, 1954

Appendix

And Jesus entered the temple and drove out all those who were buying and selling in the temple, and overturned the tables of the money changers and the seats of those who were selling doves.

— Matthew

Robby's got a quick hand.

He'll look around the room, he won't tell you his plan.

He's got a rolled cigarette hanging out his mouth, he's a cowboy kid.

Yeah, he found a six shooter gun in his dad's closet hidden with a box of fun things.

I don't even know what but he's coming for you, yeah, he's coming for you.

All the other kids with the pumped up kicks you better run, better run, outrun my gun.

All the other kids with the pumped up kicks you better run, better run faster than my bullet.

— Foster The People, "Pumped Up Kicks"

He was smiling ... That's right. You know, that, that Luke smile of his. He had it on his face right to the very end. Hell, if they didn't know it 'fore, they could tell right then that they weren't a-gonna beat him. That old Luke smile. Old Luke, he was some boy. Cool Hand Luke. Hell, he's a natural-born world-shaker.

— *Cool Hand Luke*

"What does one prefer? An art that struggles to change the social contract, but fails? Or one that seeks to please and amuse, and succeeds?"

— Robert Hughes, *The Shock of the New*

The government must suppress the fact that there is a growing anger among Indian people and that Native Americans will resist any further encroachments by the military forces of the capitalistic Americans, which is evidenced by the large number of Pine Ridge residents who took up arms on June 26, 1975 to defend themselves.

— Leonard Peltier, statement at sentencing 1977

No doubt, my name will soon be among the list of our Indian dead. At least I'll have good company — for no finer, kinder, braver, wiser, worthier men and women have ever walked this Earth than those who have already died for being Indian.

Our dead keep coming at us, a long, long line of dead, ever-growing, never-ending. To list all their names would be impossible, for the great majority died unknown, unacknowledged. Yes, the roll call of our Indian dead needs to be cried out, to be shouted from every hilltop in order to shatter the terrible silence that tries to erase the fact that we ever existed.

I would like to see a redstone wall like the blackstone wall of the Vietnam War Memorial. Yes, right there on the Mall in Washington, D.C. And on that redstone wall-pigmented with the living blood of our people (and I would happily be the first to donate that blood) — would be the names of all the Indians who ever died for being Indian. It would be dozens of times longer than the Vietnam Memorial, which celebrates the deaths of fewer than 60,000 brave lost souls. The number of our brave lost souls reaches into the many millions, and every one of them remains unquiet until this day.

Yes, the voices of Sitting Bull and Crazy Horse, of Buddy Lamont and Frank Clearwater, of Joe Stuntz and Dallas Thundershield, of Wesley Bad Heart Bull and Raymond Yellow Thunder, of Bobby Garcia and Anna Mae Aquash ... those and so, so many others. Their stilled voices cry out at us and demand to be heard.

... I have no apologies, only sorrow. I can't apologize for what I haven't done. But I can grieve, and I do. Every day, every hour, I grieve for those who died at the Oglala firefight in 1975 and for their families — for the families of FBI agents Jack Coler and Ronald Williams and, yes, for the family of Joe Killright Stuntz — a 21-year old brave-hearted Indian whose death from a bullet at Oglala that same day, like the deaths of hundreds of other Indians at Pine Ridge at that terrible time, has never been investigated. My heart aches in remembering the suffering and fear under which so many of my people were forced to live at that time, the very suffering and fear that brought me and the others to Oglala that day — to defend the defenseless.

— Leonard Peltier, "My Life is My Sundance"

We guard our world with locks and guns
And we guard our fine possessions
And once a year when Christmas comes
We give to our relations
And perhaps we give a little to the poor
If the generosity should seize us
But if any one of us should interfere
In the business of why they are poor
They get the same as the rebel Jesus   — Jackson Browne

In the old days class warfare was between the rich and the poor, and that's the kind of class war I can sink my teeth into.

— Joe Bageant

But during those 33 years Jesus planted a doctrine, which without a doubt is revolutionary, without a doubt. One must read the real Jesus, not the Jesus of the oligarchy or the Jesus of the elite, the real Jesus: the one who was born there among the poor, who was a poor boy, who grew up among the poor, who stood up to the Roman imperialism of those times, who stood up to the religious elite of those times, who went around encouraging people to love one another.

— Hugo Chavez

As long as you fight, nobody know how the fight gonna come out. There's a possibility I might win, but I know if I stop I cannot win. One man can make a difference, if he's sincere.

— Ruchell McGee, Marin County Courthouse Rebellion

"I'm going to do my job and I believe that I was born not to die in a car wreck. I don't believe I'm going to die slipping on a piece of ice. I don't believe I was born to die because of a bad heart. I don't believe I was born to die of lung cancer. I believe I'm going to be able to do what I came to do. I believe that I'm going to be able to die high off the people. I believe that I will be able to die as a revolutionary in the international revolutionary proletariat struggle. And I hope that each one of you will be able to live in it. I think that struggles are going to come. Why don't you live for the people? Why don't you live for the struggle? Why don't you die for the struggle?

— Fred Hampton

Tʜᴇ Eɴᴅ

We call upon all the conscientious citizens of America to assist us in putting an end to the situation which threatens the lives of not only us, but every one of you.

— L.D. Barkley, a leader of Attica rebellion, killed when guards and police stormed the prison yard, Sept. 13, 1971, 9:46 a.m.

I always say that people who are colored will one day rule this planet.

— Floyd Looks For Buffalo Hand

ALLISON HEALY - ARTIST

Raised in the Northwoods of Minnesota, Allison developed a deep connection to the natural world as well as a great attention to detail, a theme that carries through much of her work. She left high school two years early and received an associate degree in liberal arts, with a focus in literature and fine art at the age of eighteen. Earning a Bachelor of Fine Arts degree in illustration from the Minneapolis College of Art & Design, she also spent some time abroad intensively studying illustration and graphic design at the University of Brighton, on the south coast of England. Her work has appeared on a range of publications, including but not limited to: book covers, children's books, magazines, album covers, greeting cards, and several applied graphics for various products. She is currently living and working in Boston, Massachusetts, where her studio is now based.

www.ingramcontent.com/pod-product-compliance
Lightning Source LLC
Chambersburg PA
CBHW060811120626
46557CB00001B/178